STINKY

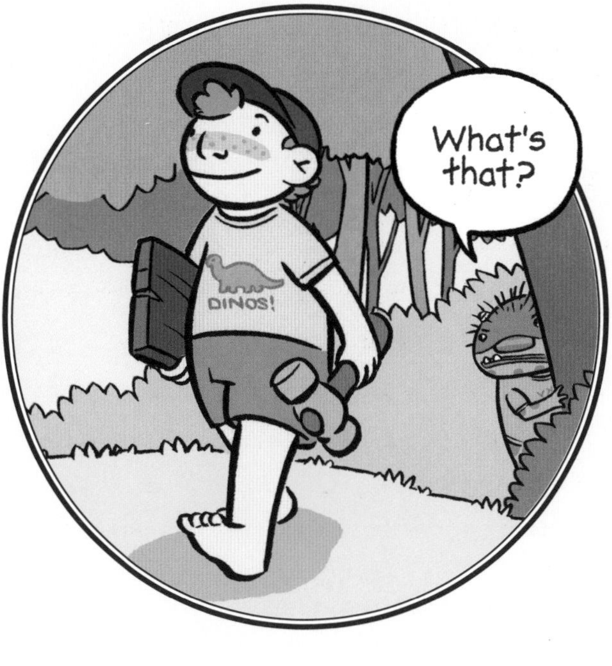
What's that?
DINOS!

A TOON BOOK BY

ELEANOR DAVIS

TOON BOOKS, NEW YORK

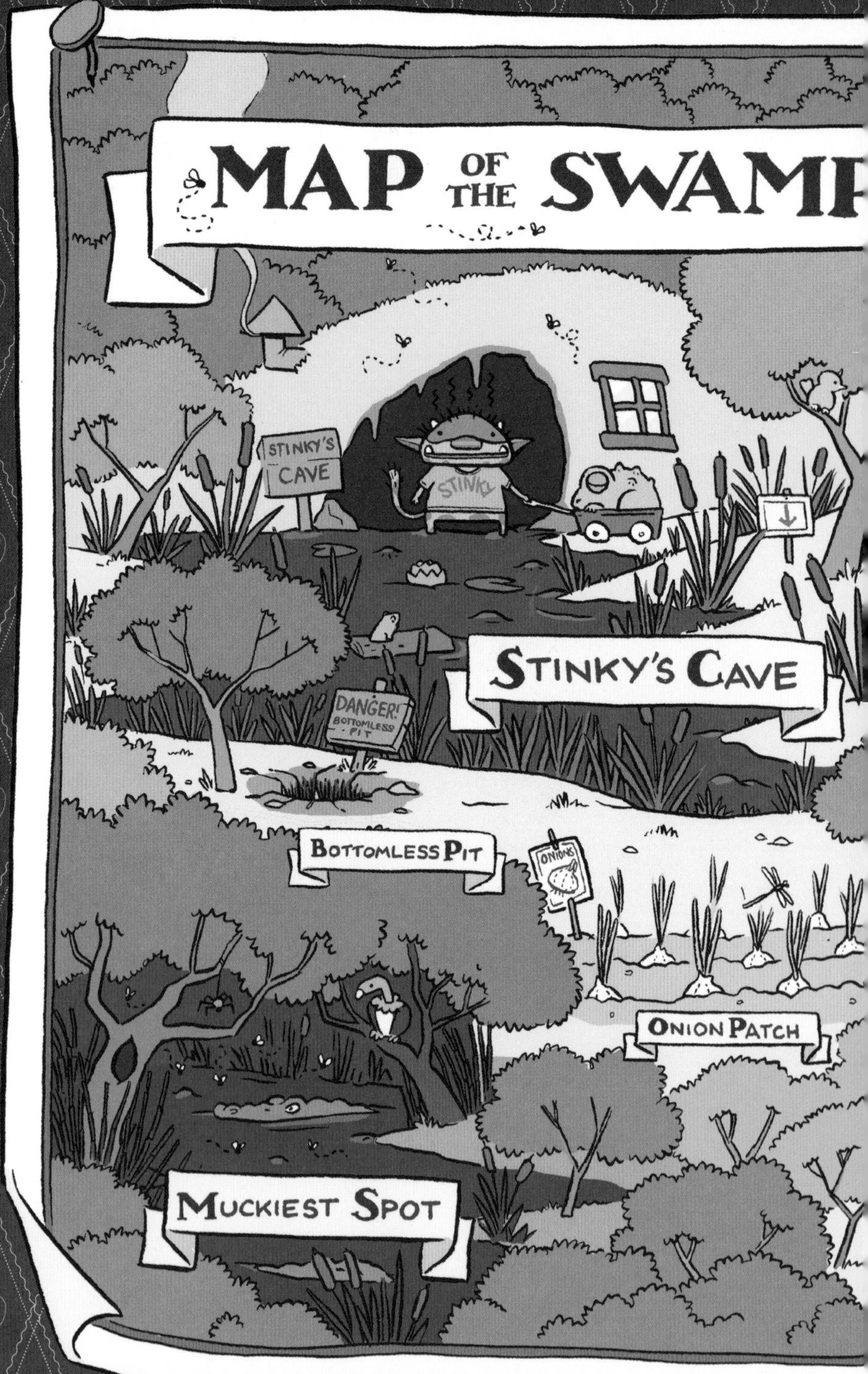
MAP OF THE SWAMP
STINKY'S CAVE
STINKY
STINKY'S CAVE
DANGER! BOTTOMLESS PIT
BOTTOMLESS PIT
ONIONS
ONION PATCH
MUCKIEST SPOT

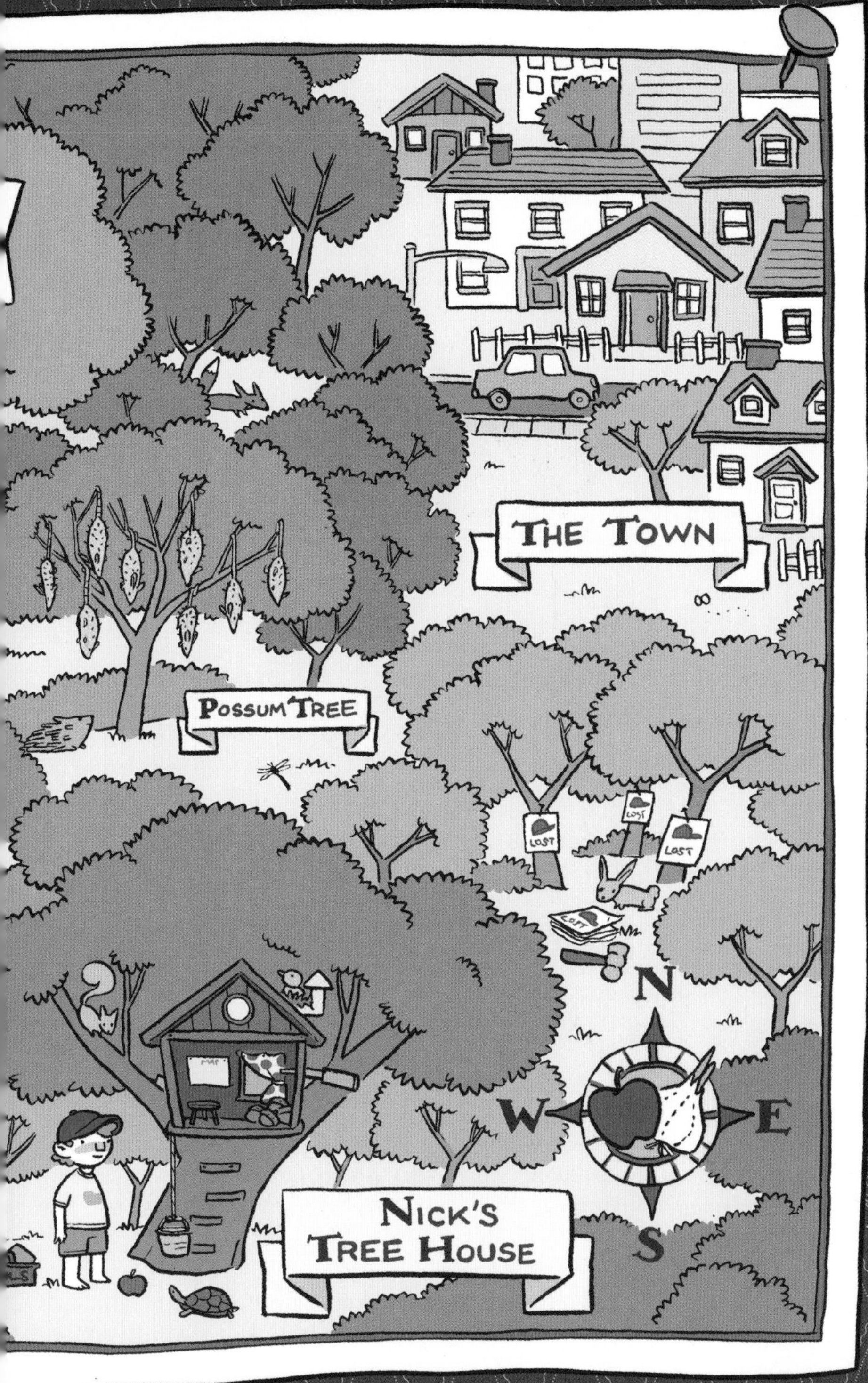
THE TOWN
POSSUM TREE
LOST
LOST
LOST
N
W
E
S
NICK'S TREE HOUSE

A THEODOR SEUSS GEISEL HONOR BOOK 2009
BOOKLIST'S NOTABLE CHILDREN'S BOOKS 2009
BANK STREET COLLEGE OF EDUCATION'S
BEST CHILDREN'S BOOKS OF THE YEAR 2009
ALSC GRAPHIC NOVELS READING LIST 2014

Editorial Director: FRANÇOISE MOULY

Book Design: FRANÇOISE MOULY & JONATHAN BENNETT

ELEANOR DAVIS' artwork was drawn in pen and ink and colored digitally.

A TOON Book™ © 2008 Eleanor Davis & RAW Junior, LLC, 27 Greene Street, New York, NY 10013. TOON Books®, TOON Graphics™, LITTLE LIT® and TOON Into Reading™ are trademarks of RAW Junior, LLC. All rights reserved. No part of this book may be used or reproduced in any manner whatsoever without written permission except in the case of brief quotations embodied in critical articles and reviews. All our books are Smyth Sewn (the highest library-quality binding available) and printed with soy-based inks on acid-free woodfree paper harvested from responsible sources. Printed in China by C&C Offset Printing Co., Ltd. Distributed to the trade by Consortium Book Sales & Distribution, a division of Ingram Content Group; orders (866) 400-5351; ips@ingramcontent.com; www.cbsd.com.
Library of Congress Control Number: 2007943857.

ISBN 978-0-979923-84-5 (hardcover)

ISBN 978-1-943145-40-9 (paperback)

20 21 22 23 24 25 C&C 12 11 10 9 8 7 6 5

www.TOON-BOOKS.com

CHAPTER ONE

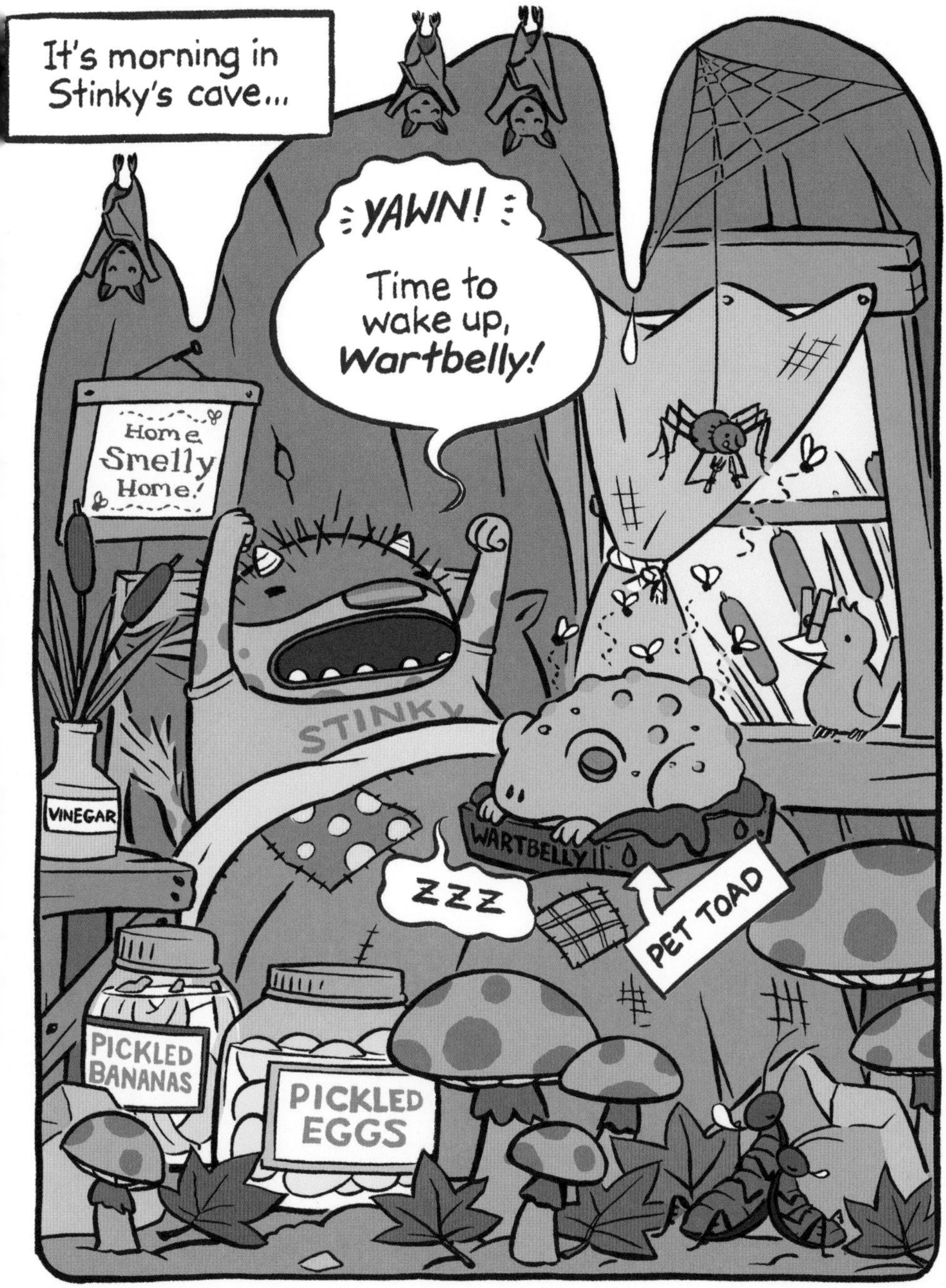
It's morning in Stinky's cave...
YAWN!
Time to wake up, Wartbelly!
Home Smelly Home!
VINEGAR
STINKY
WARTBELLY
ZZZ
PET TOAD
PICKLED BANANAS
PICKLED EGGS

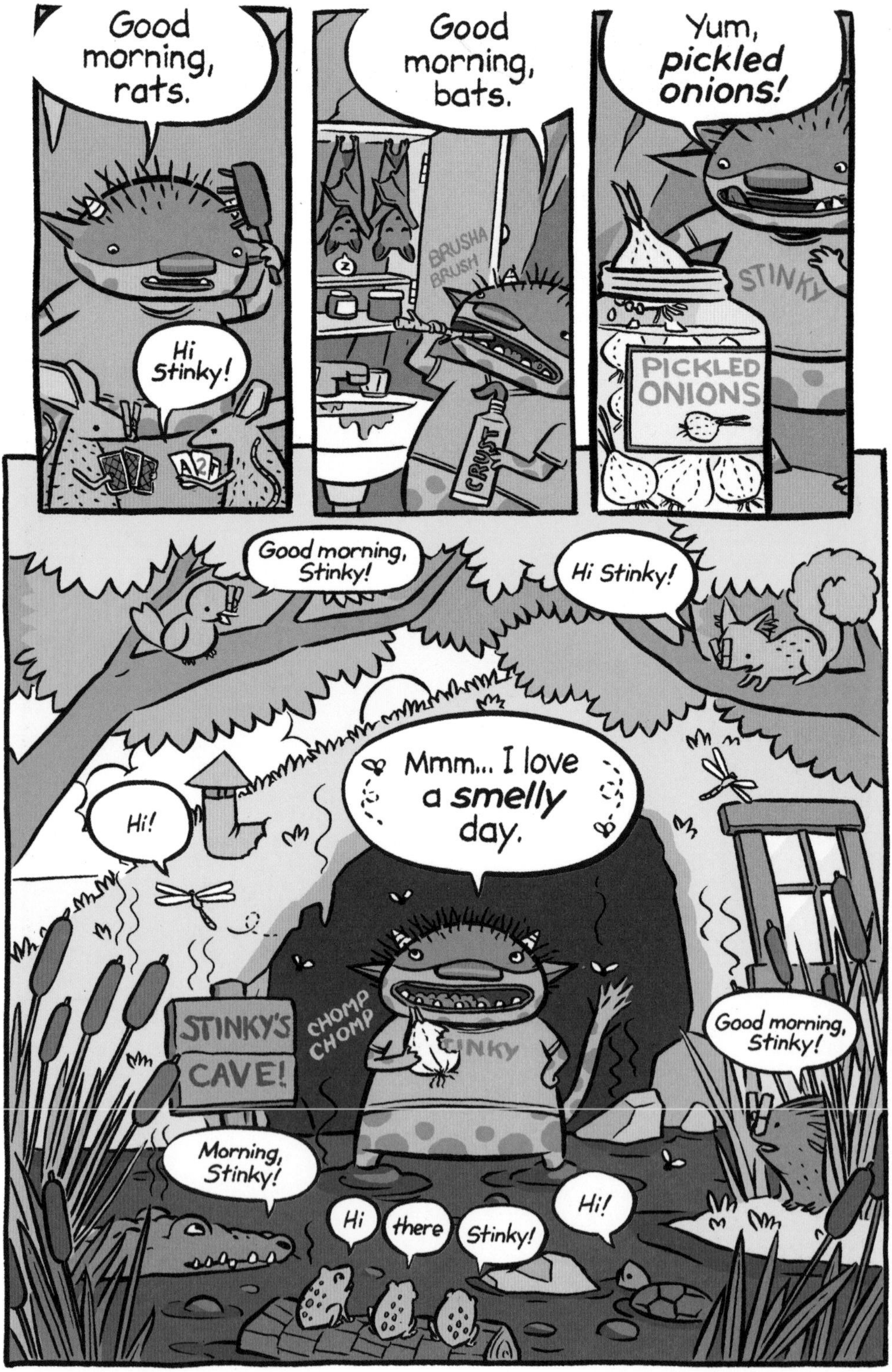
Good morning, rats.
Hi Stinky!
Good morning, bats.
BRUSHA BRUSH
CRUST
Yum, *pickled onions!*
PICKLED ONIONS
STINKY
Good morning, Stinky!
Hi Stinky!
Hi!
Mmm... I love a *smelly* day.
STINKY'S CAVE!
CHOMP CHOMP
Good morning, Stinky!
Morning, Stinky!
Hi
there
Stinky!
Hi!

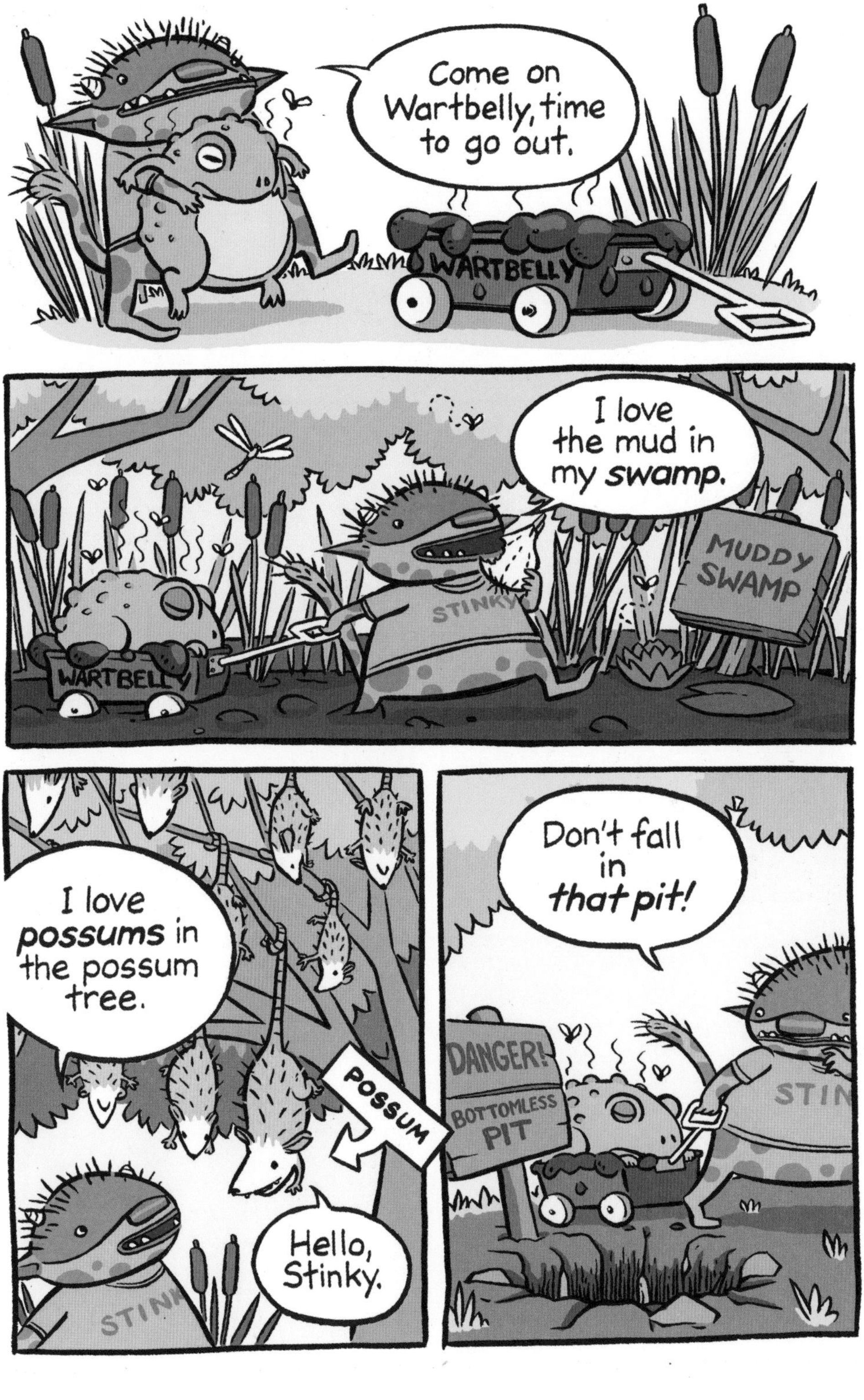
Come on Wartbelly, time to go out.
WARTBELLY
I love the mud in my *swamp.*
MUDDY SWAMP
I love *possums* in the possum tree.
POSSUM
Hello, Stinky.
Don't fall in *that pit!*
DANGER!
BOTTOMLESS PIT

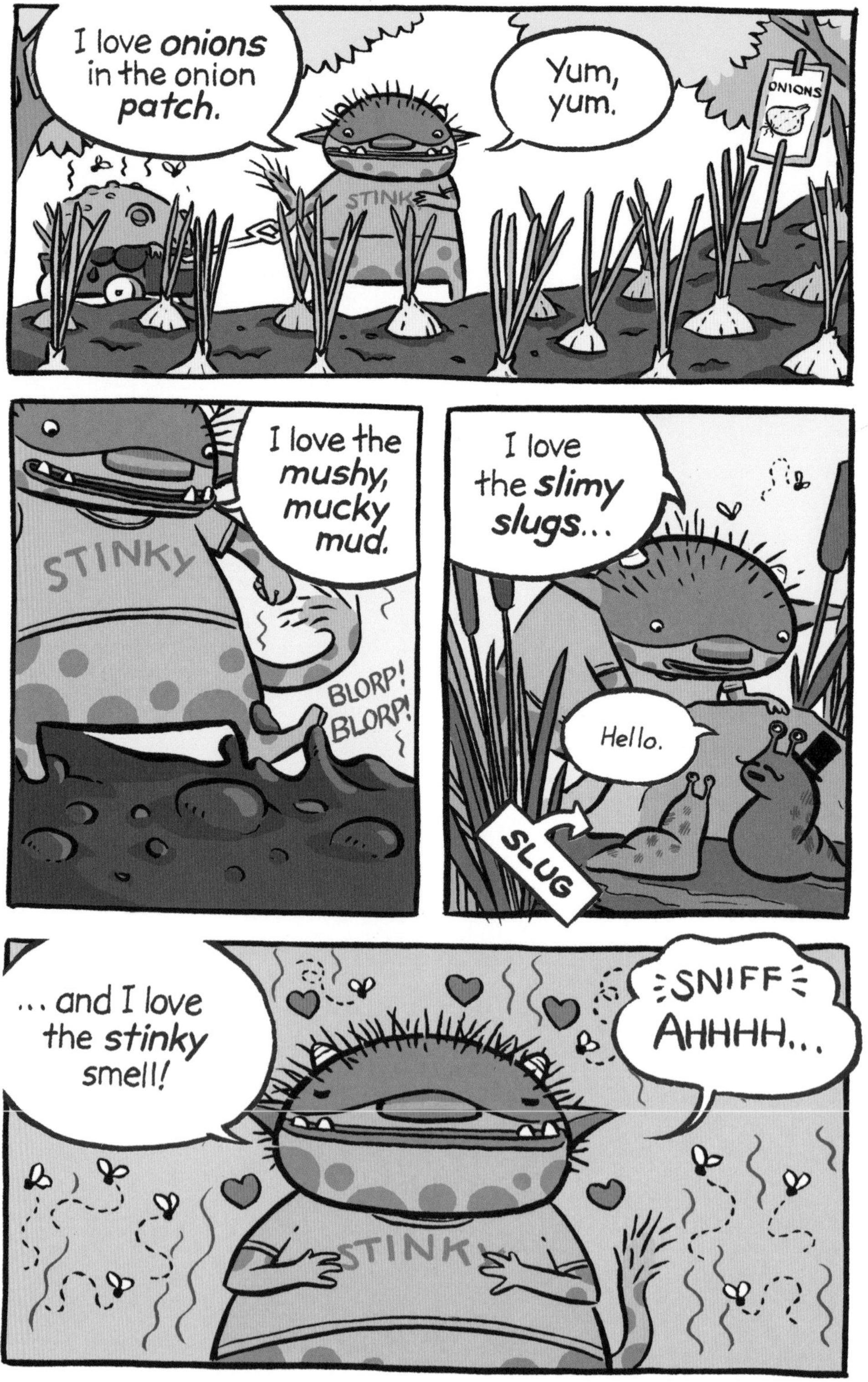
I love onions in the onion patch.
Yum, yum.
ONIONS
STINKY
I love the mushy, mucky mud.
STINKY
BLORP! BLORP!
I love the slimy slugs...
Hello.
SLUG
... and I love the stinky smell!
SNIFF AHHHH...
STINKY

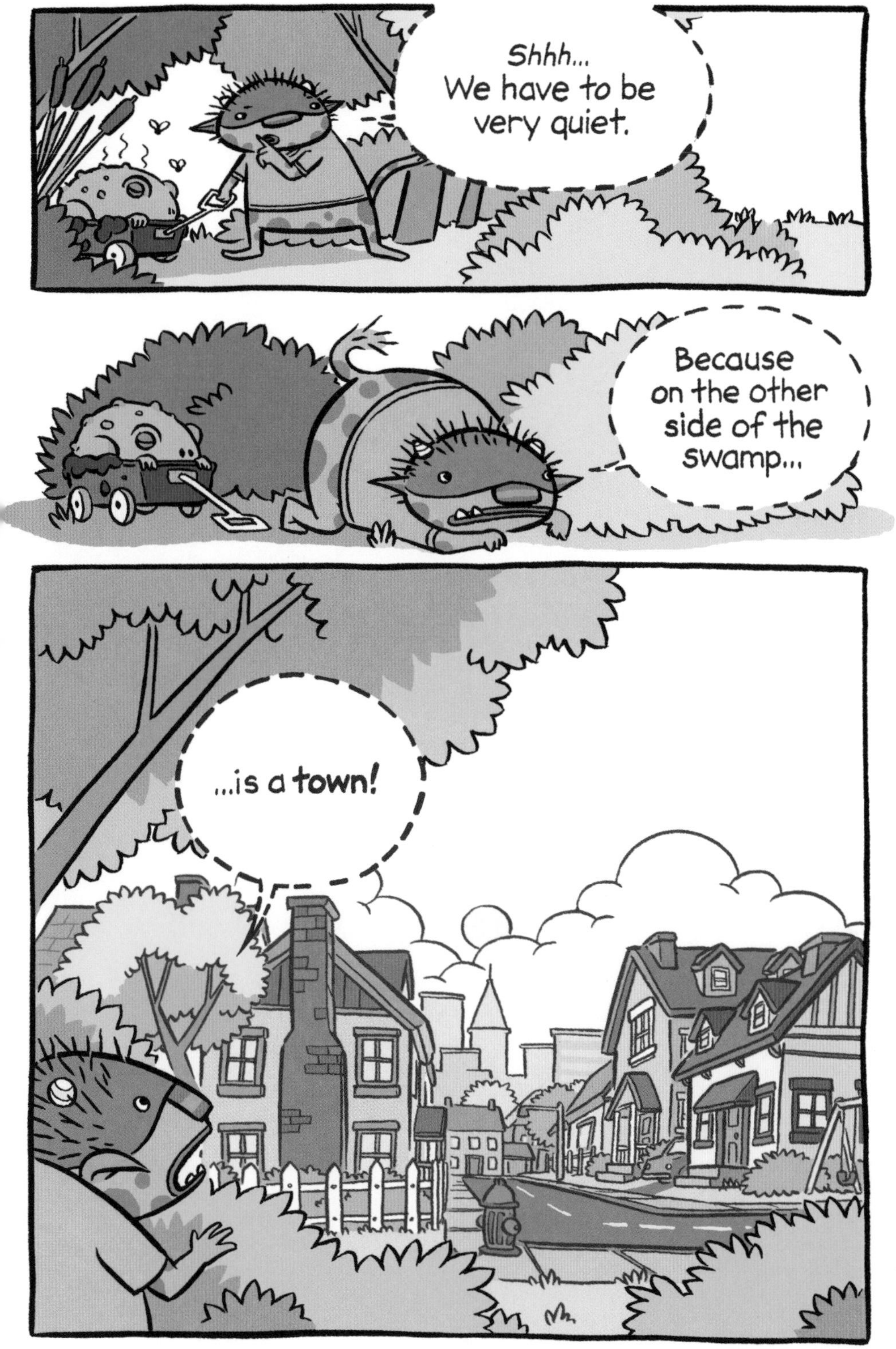
Shhh... We have to be very quiet.
Because on the other side of the swamp...
...is a town!

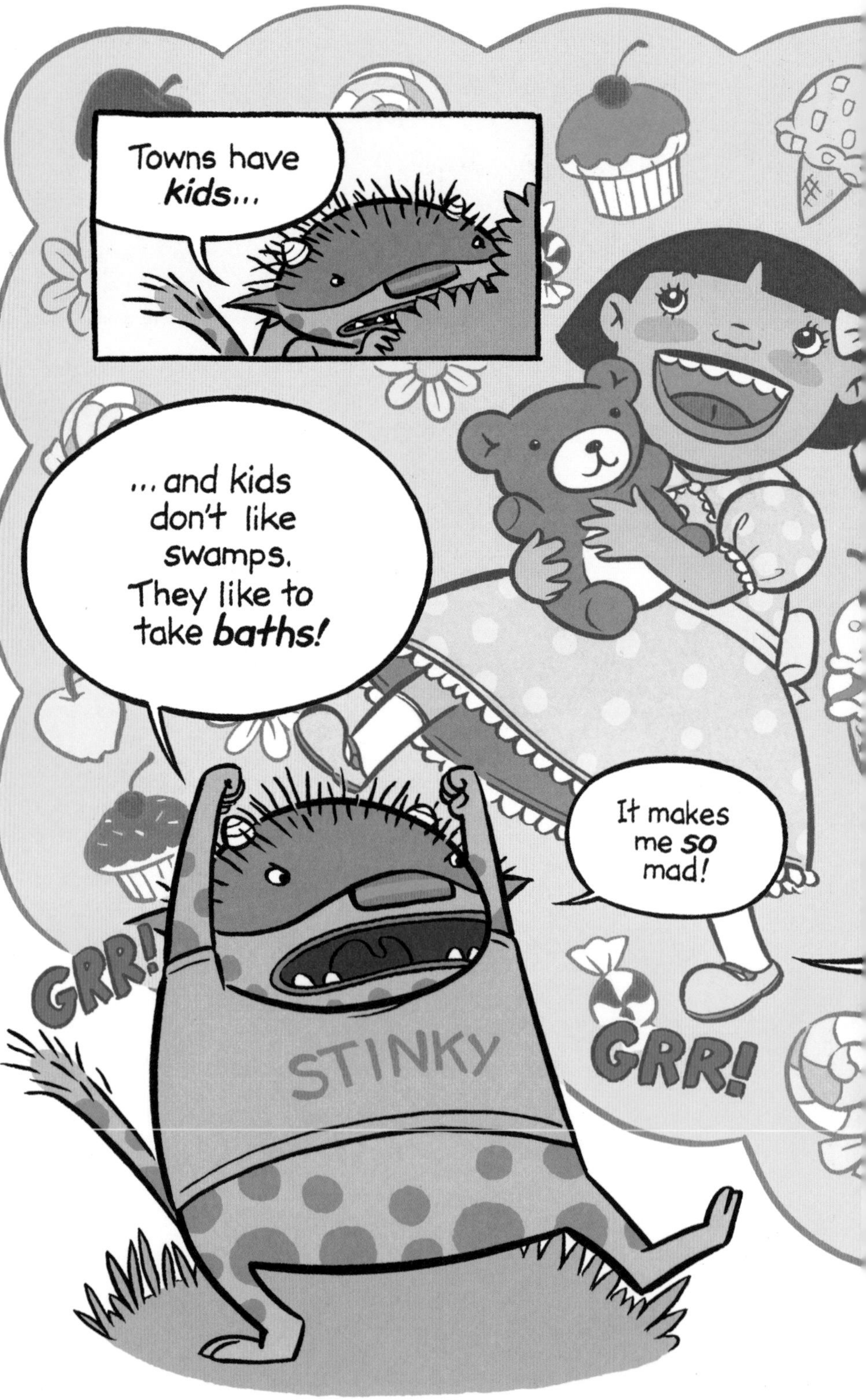
Towns have *kids*...
...and kids don't like swamps. They like to take ***baths!***
It makes me ***so*** mad!
GRR!
GRR!
STINKY

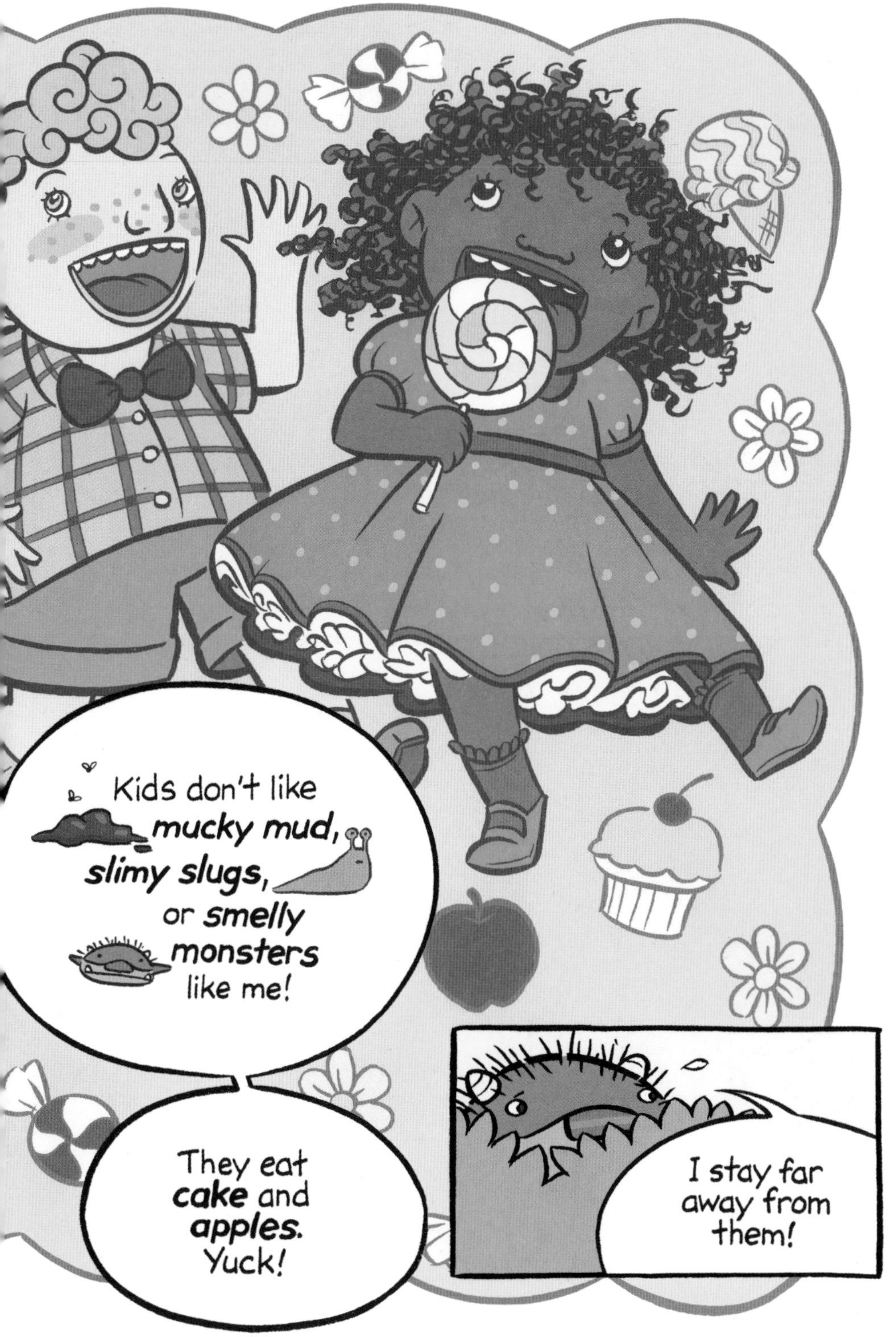

Kids don't like **mucky mud**, **slimy slugs**, or **smelly monsters** like me!
They eat **cake** and **apples.** Yuck!
I stay far away from them!

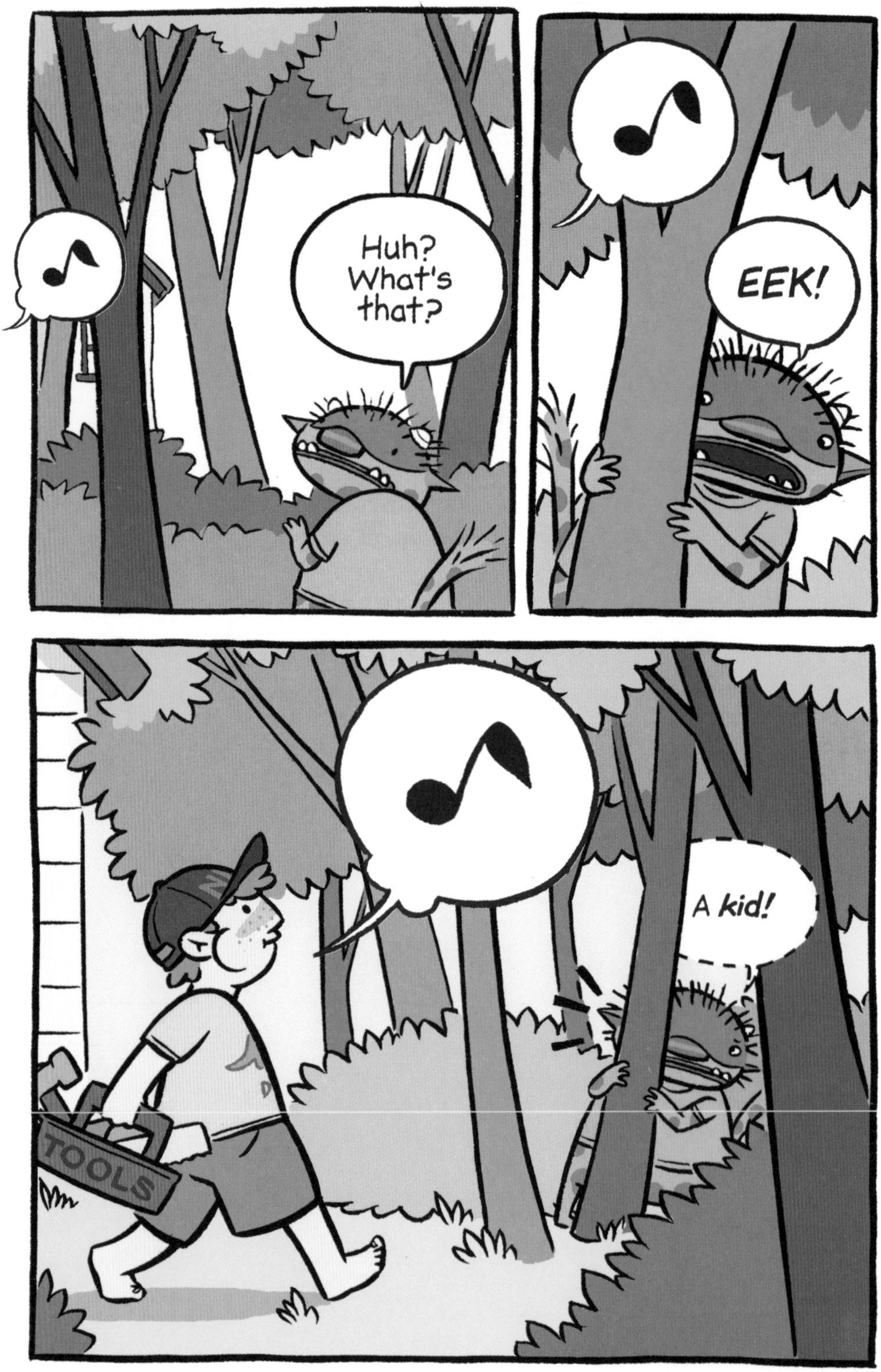
Huh? What's that?
EEK!
A kid!
TOOLS

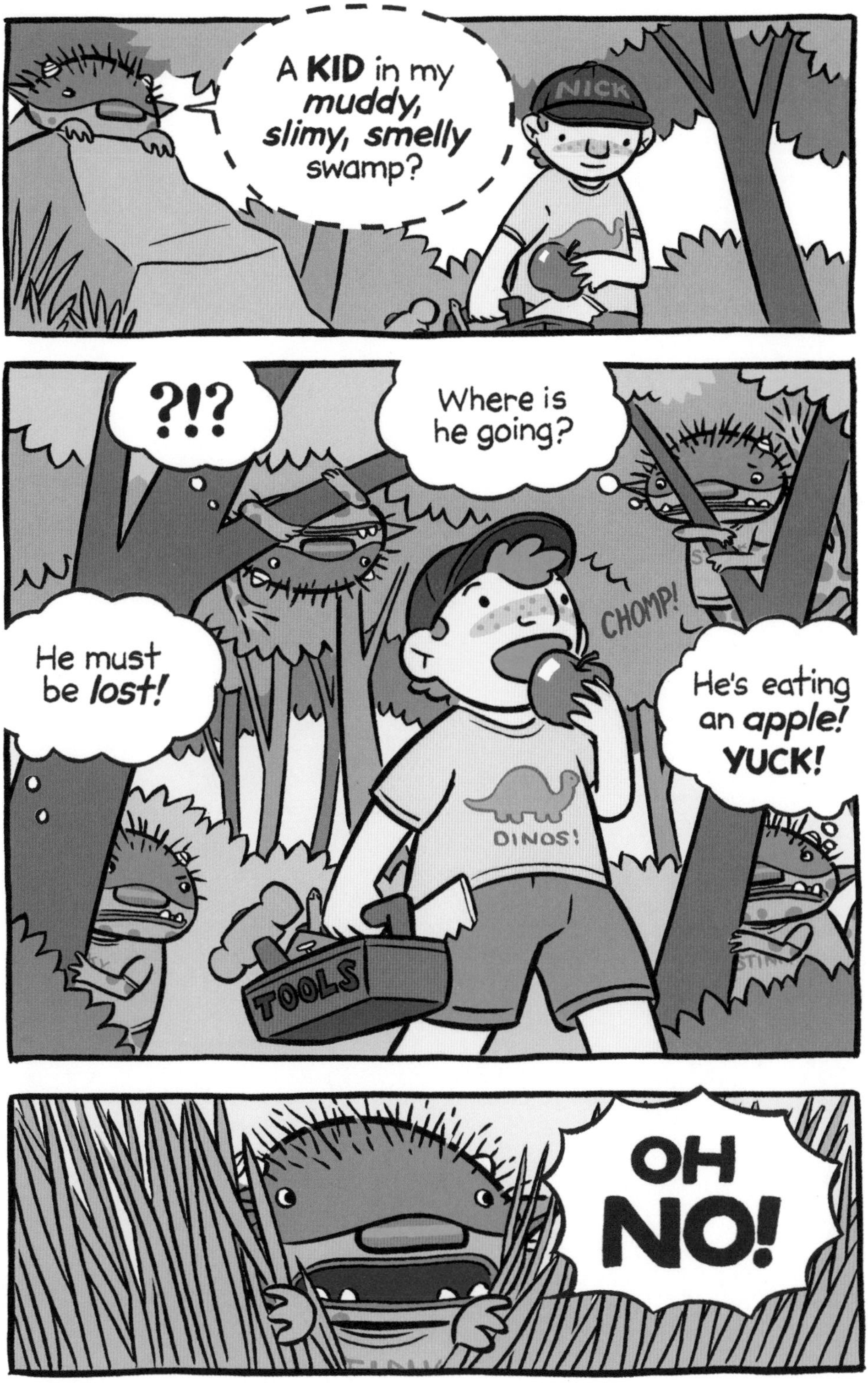
A KID in my muddy, slimy, smelly swamp?
NICK
?!?
Where is he going?
CHOMP!
He must be lost!
He's eating an apple! YUCK!
DINOS!
TOOLS
OH NO!

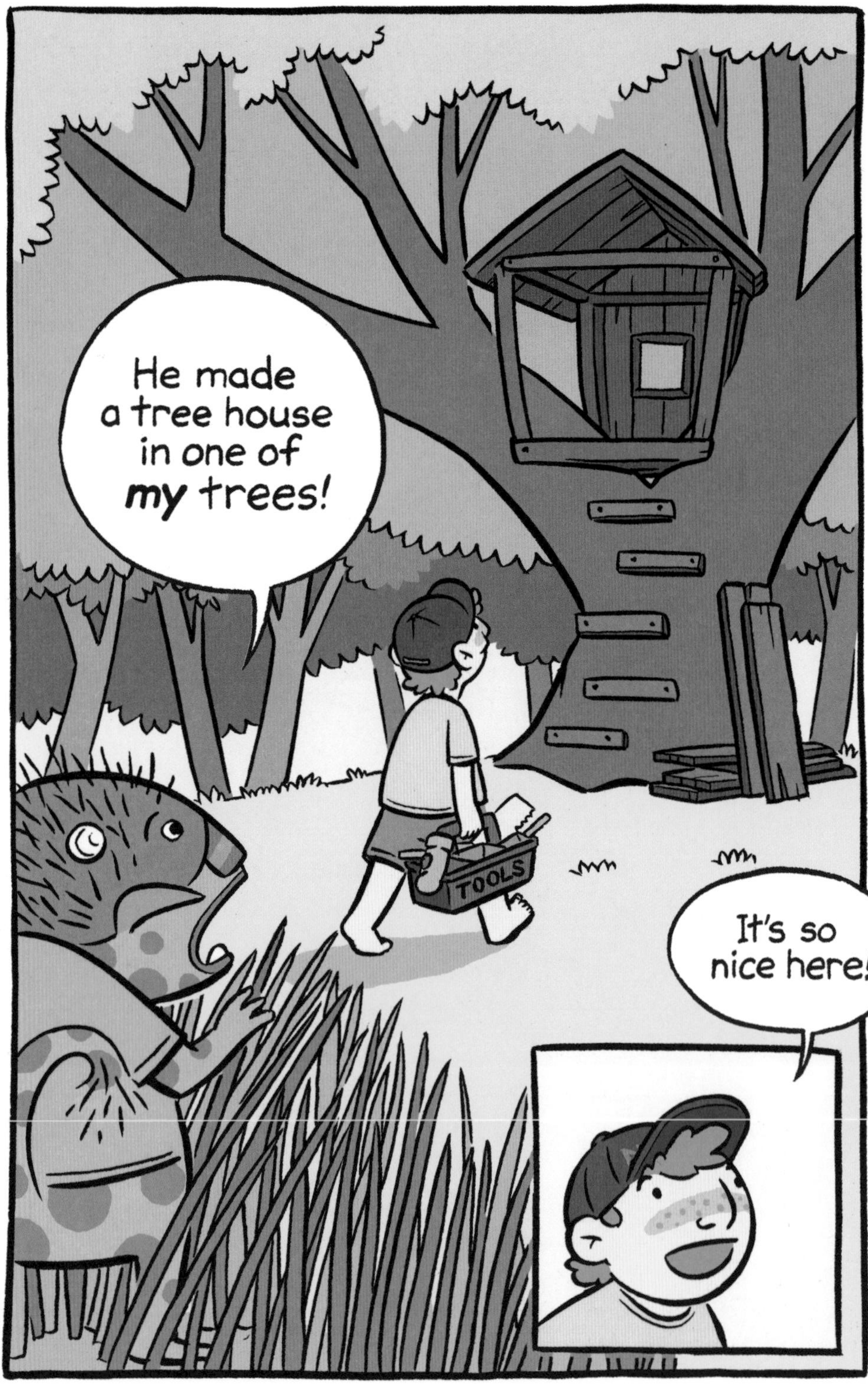
He made a tree house in one of *my* trees!
TOOLS
It's so nice here!

CHAPTER TWO

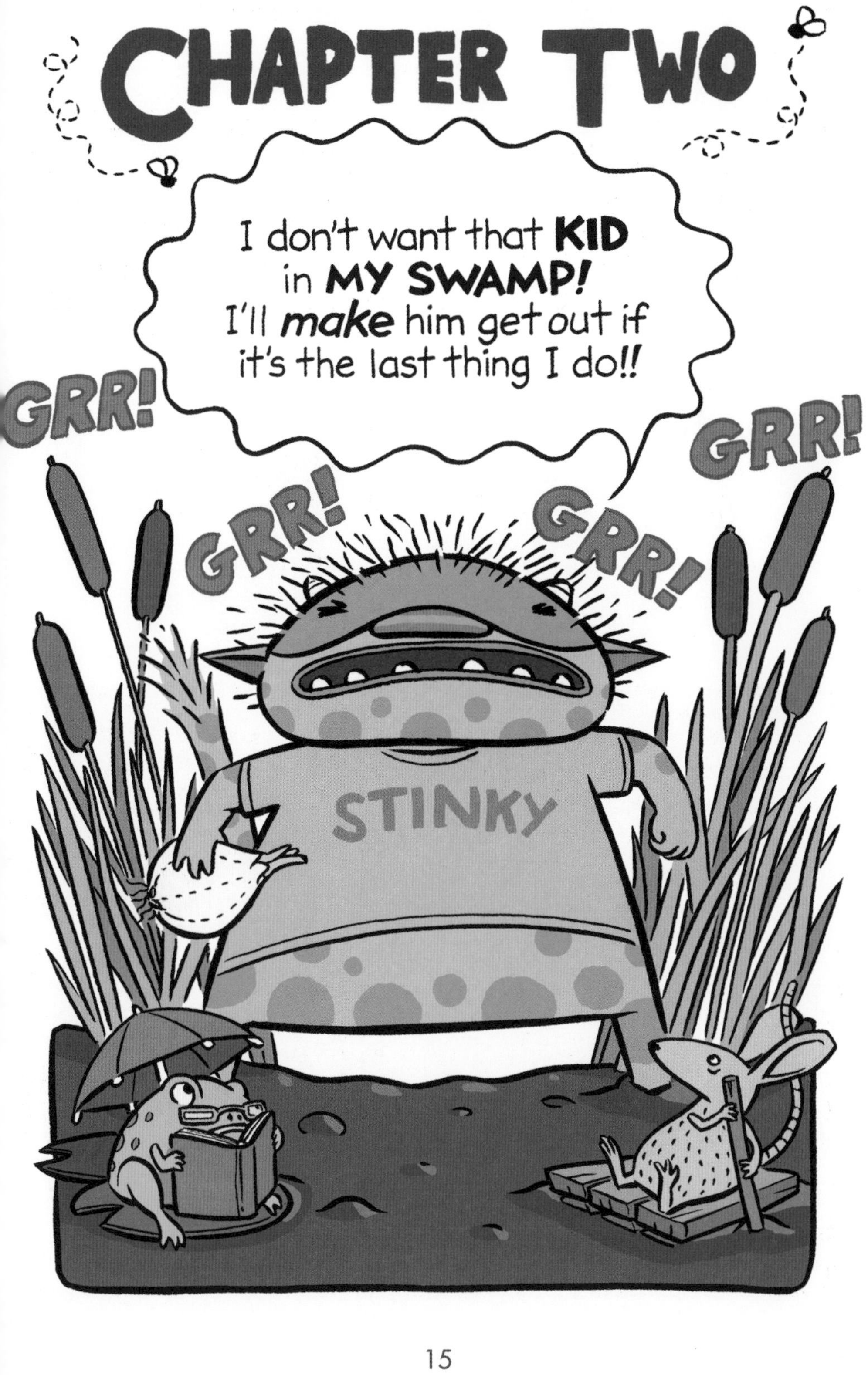
I don't want that **KID** in **MY SWAMP!** I'll *make* him get out if it's the last thing I do!!
GRR!
GRR!
GRR!
GRR!
STINKY

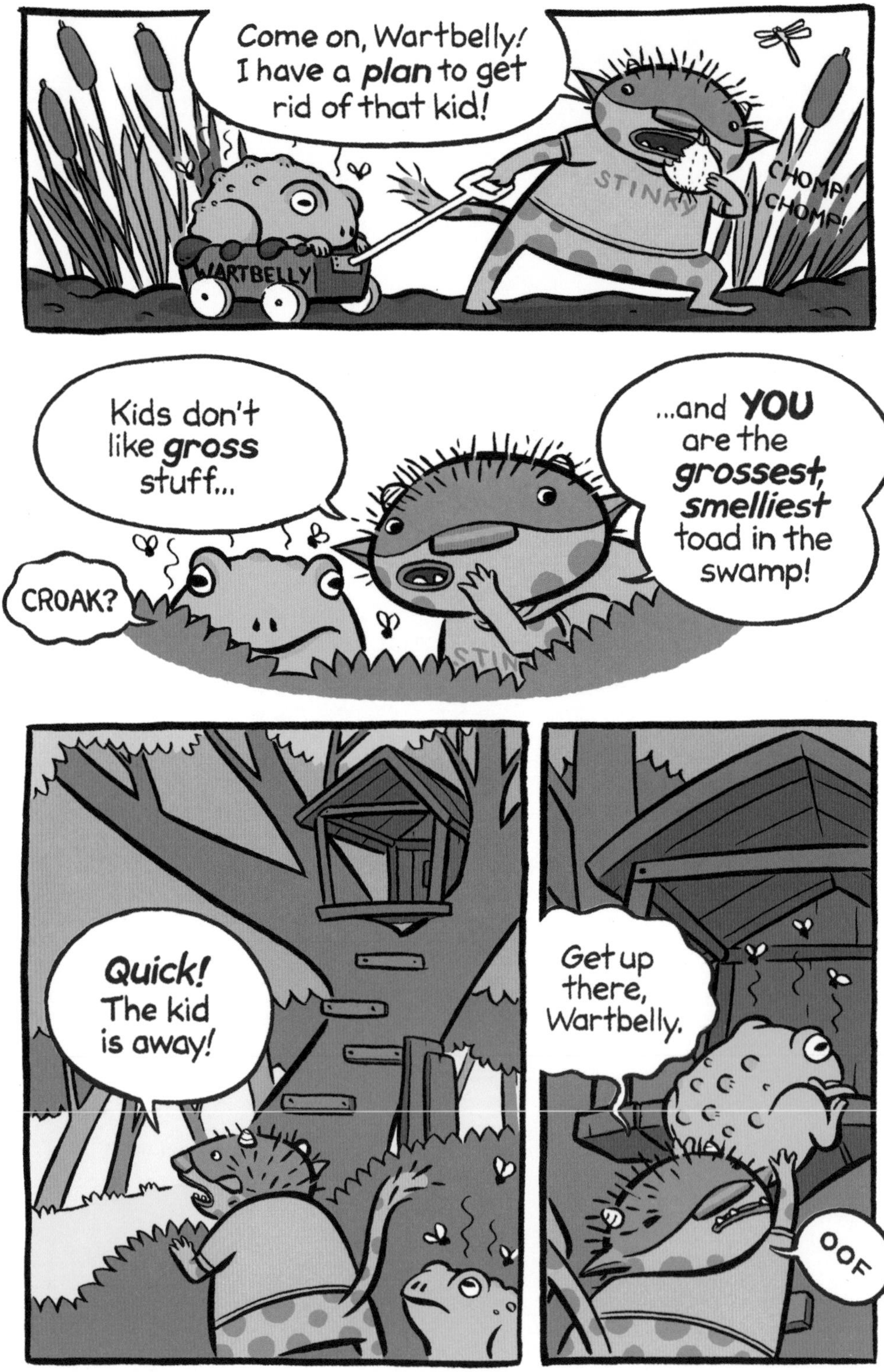
Come on, Wartbelly! I have a plan to get rid of that kid!
WARTBELLY
STINKY
CHOMP! CHOMP!
Kids don't like gross stuff...
...and YOU are the grossest, smelliest toad in the swamp!
CROAK?
Quick! The kid is away!
Get up there, Wartbelly.
OOF

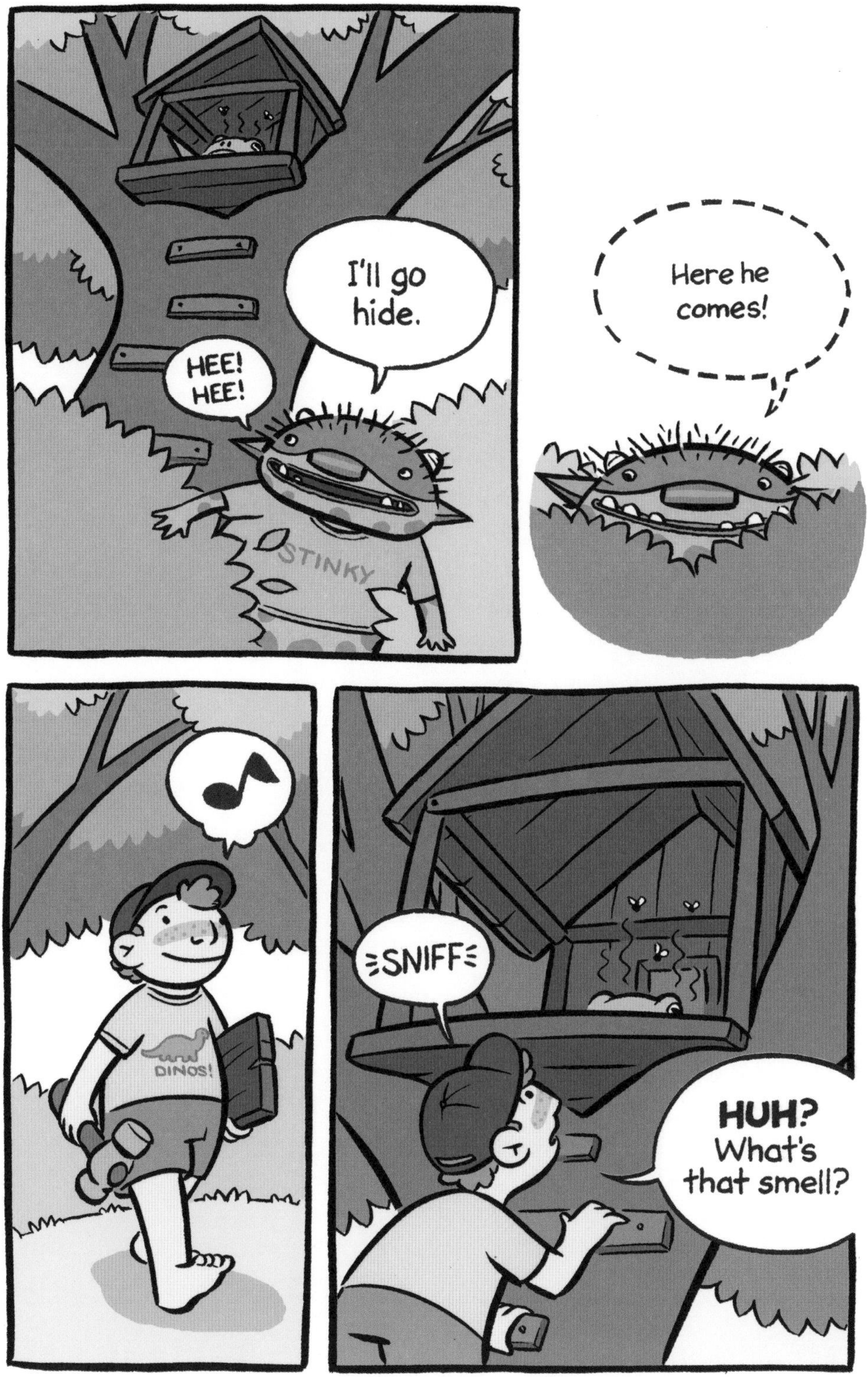
I'll go hide.
HEE! HEE!
STINKY
Here he comes!
DINOS!
SNIFF
HUH? What's that smell?

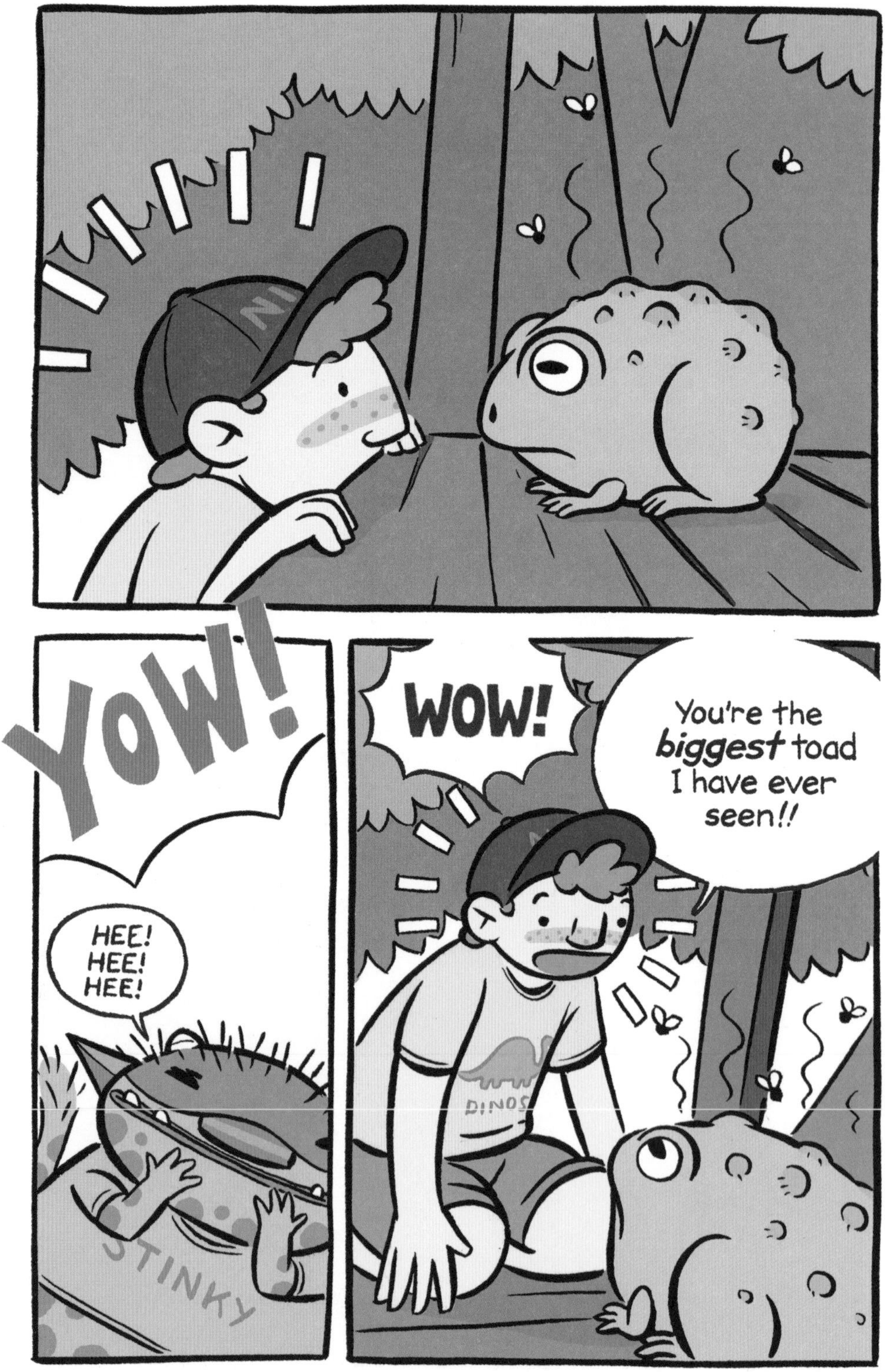
YOW!
HEE! HEE! HEE!
STINKY
WOW!
You're the **biggest** toad I have ever seen!!
DINOS

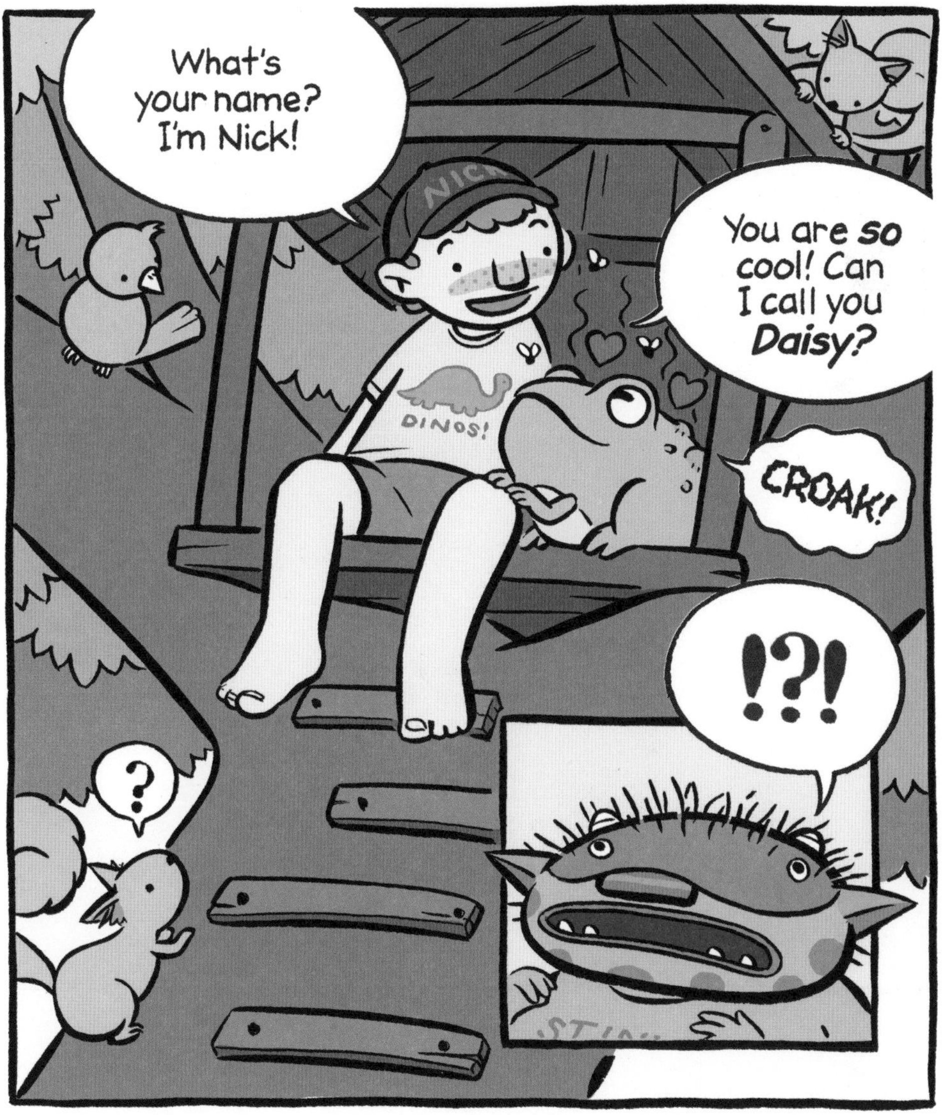
What's your name? I'm Nick!
NICK
You are **so** cool! Can I call you ***Daisy?***
DINOS!
CROAK!
?
!?!

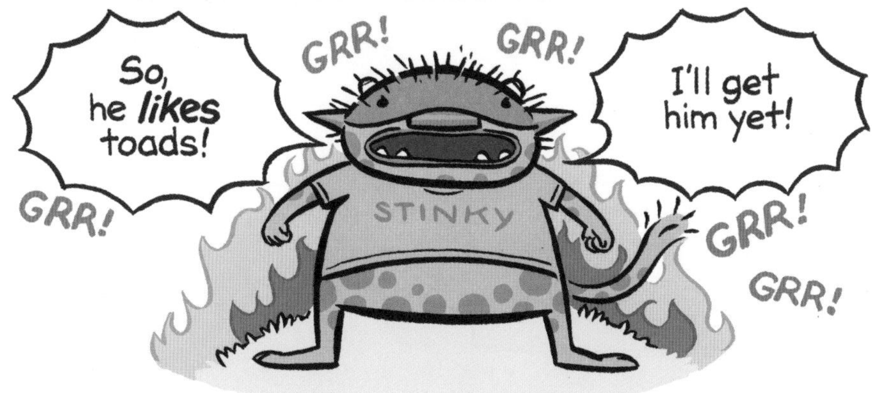
So, he ***likes*** toads!
GRR!
GRR!
I'll get him yet!
GRR!
STINKY
GRR!
GRR!

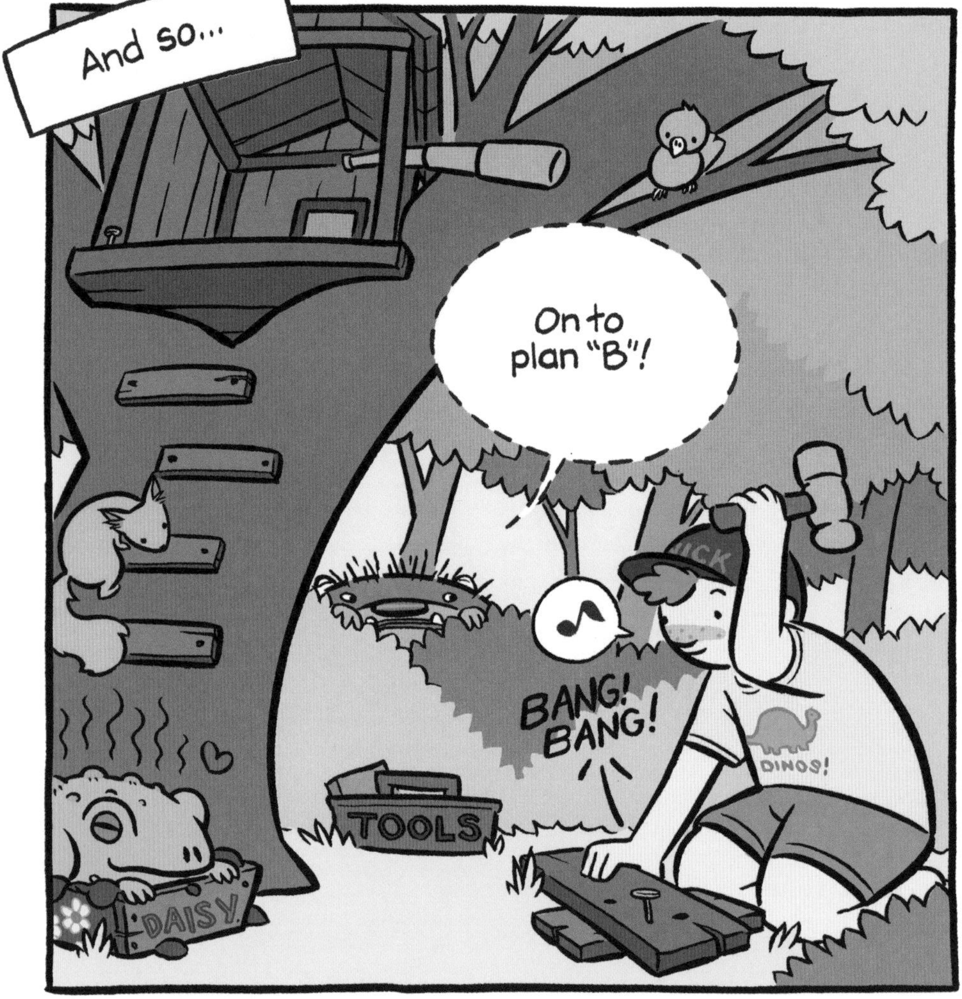
And so...
On to plan "B"!
BANG! BANG!
TOOLS
DAISY
DINOS!

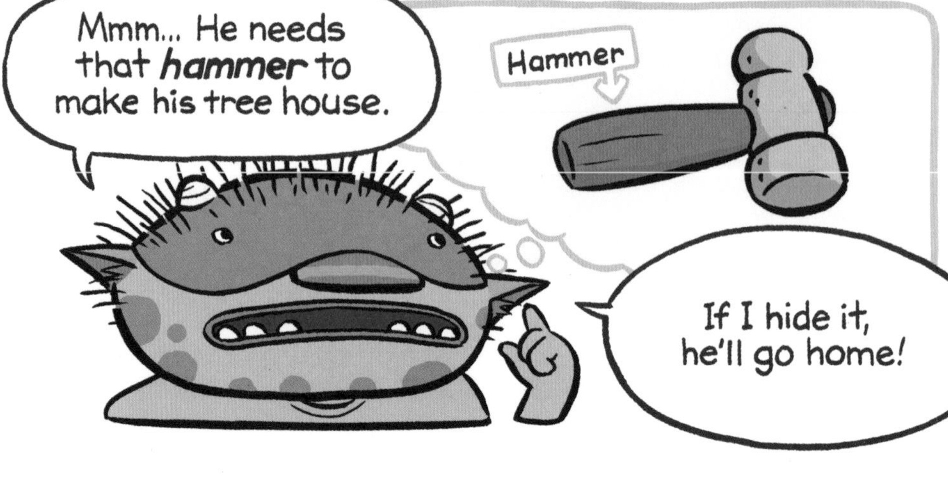
Mmm... He needs that ***hammer*** to make his tree house.
Hammer
If I hide it, he'll go home!

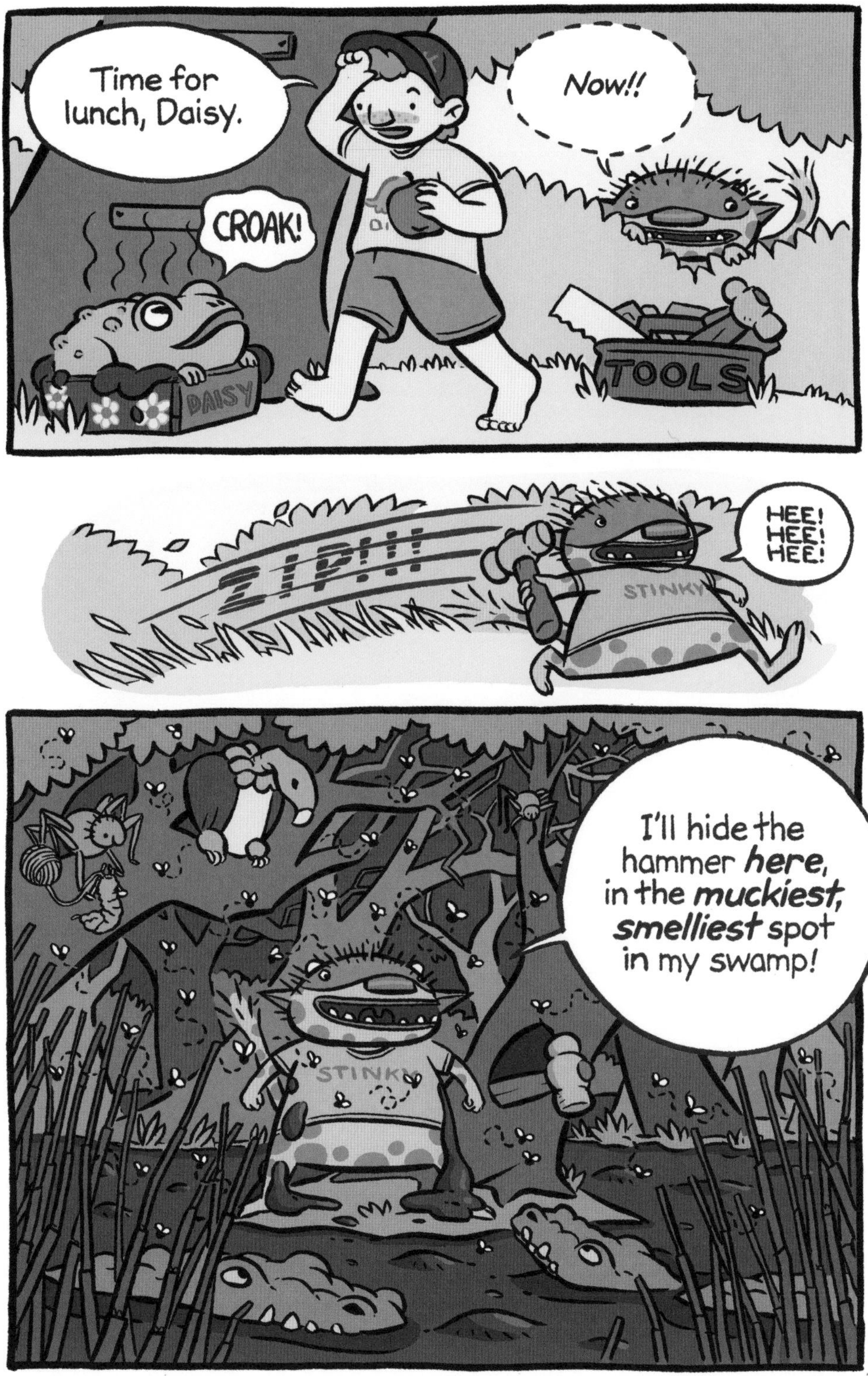
Time for lunch, Daisy.
CROAK!
DAISY
Now!!
TOOLS
ZIP!!!
STINKY
HEE! HEE! HEE!
I'll hide the hammer *here*, in the *muckiest, smelliest* spot in my swamp!
STINKY

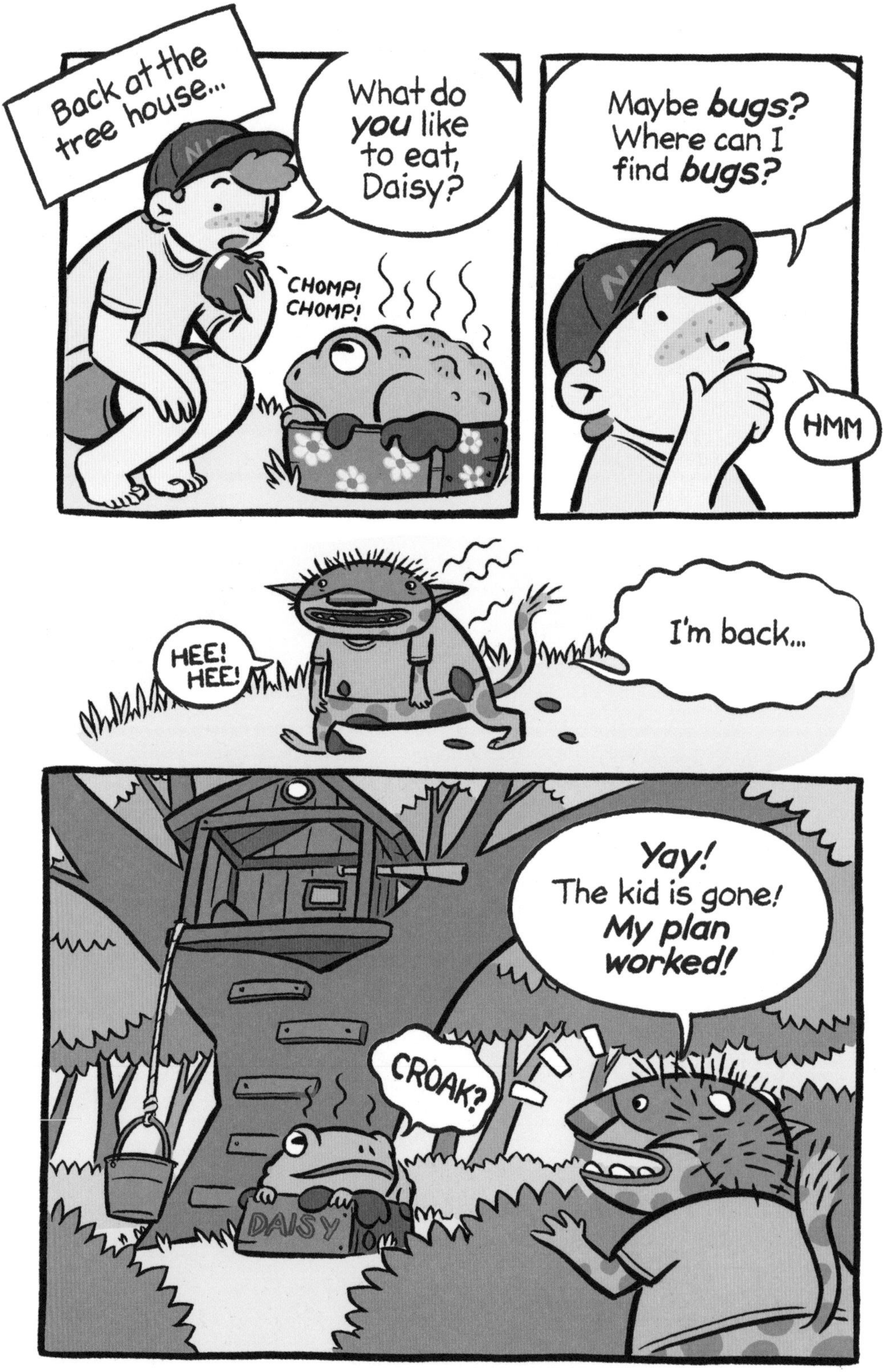
Back at the tree house...
What do you like to eat, Daisy?
CHOMP! CHOMP!
Maybe bugs? Where can I find bugs?
HMM
HEE! HEE!
I'm back...
Yay! The kid is gone! My plan worked!
CROAK?
DAISY

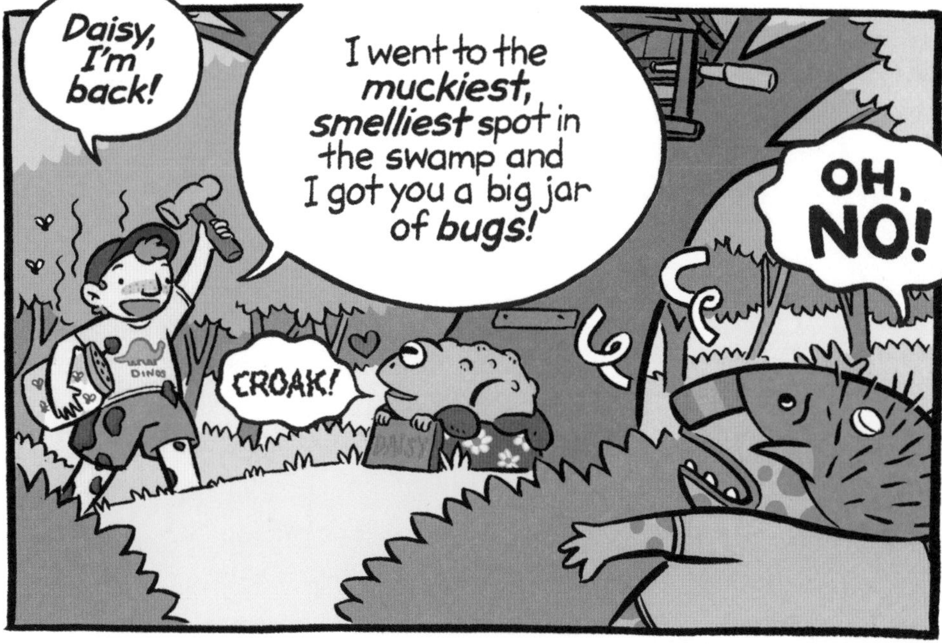
Daisy, I'm back!
I went to the muckiest, smelliest spot in the swamp and I got you a big jar of bugs!
OH, NO!
CROAK!
DINOS
DAISY

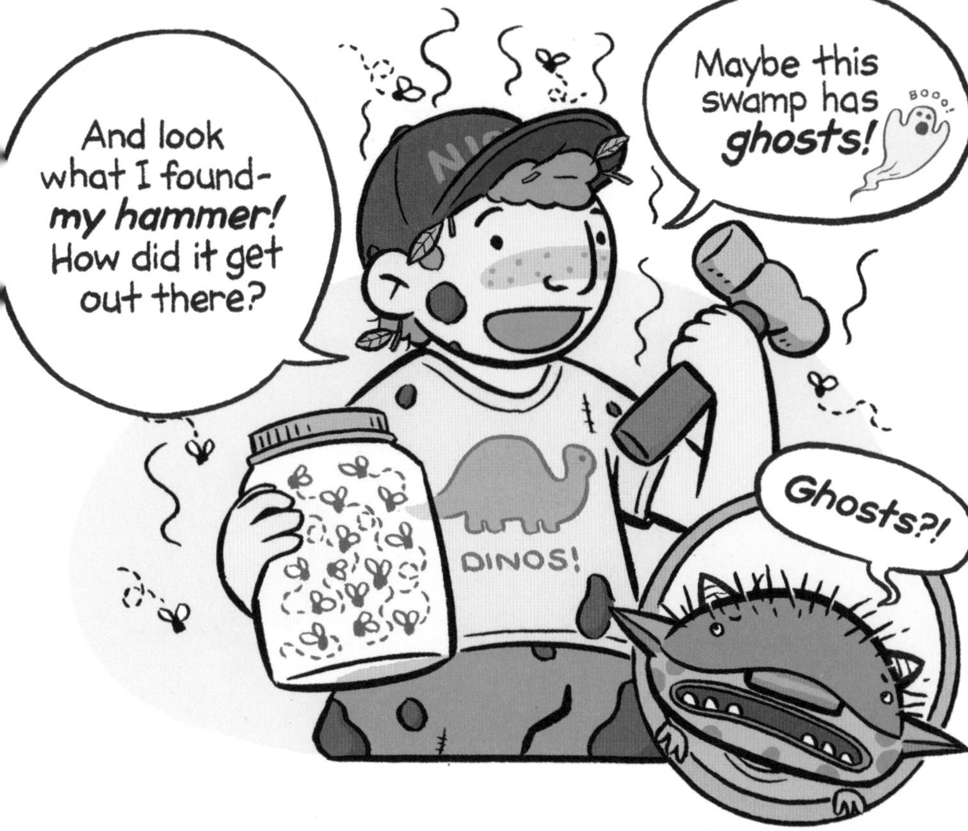
And look what I found- my hammer! How did it get out there?
Maybe this swamp has ghosts!
BOOO!
DINOS!
Ghosts?!

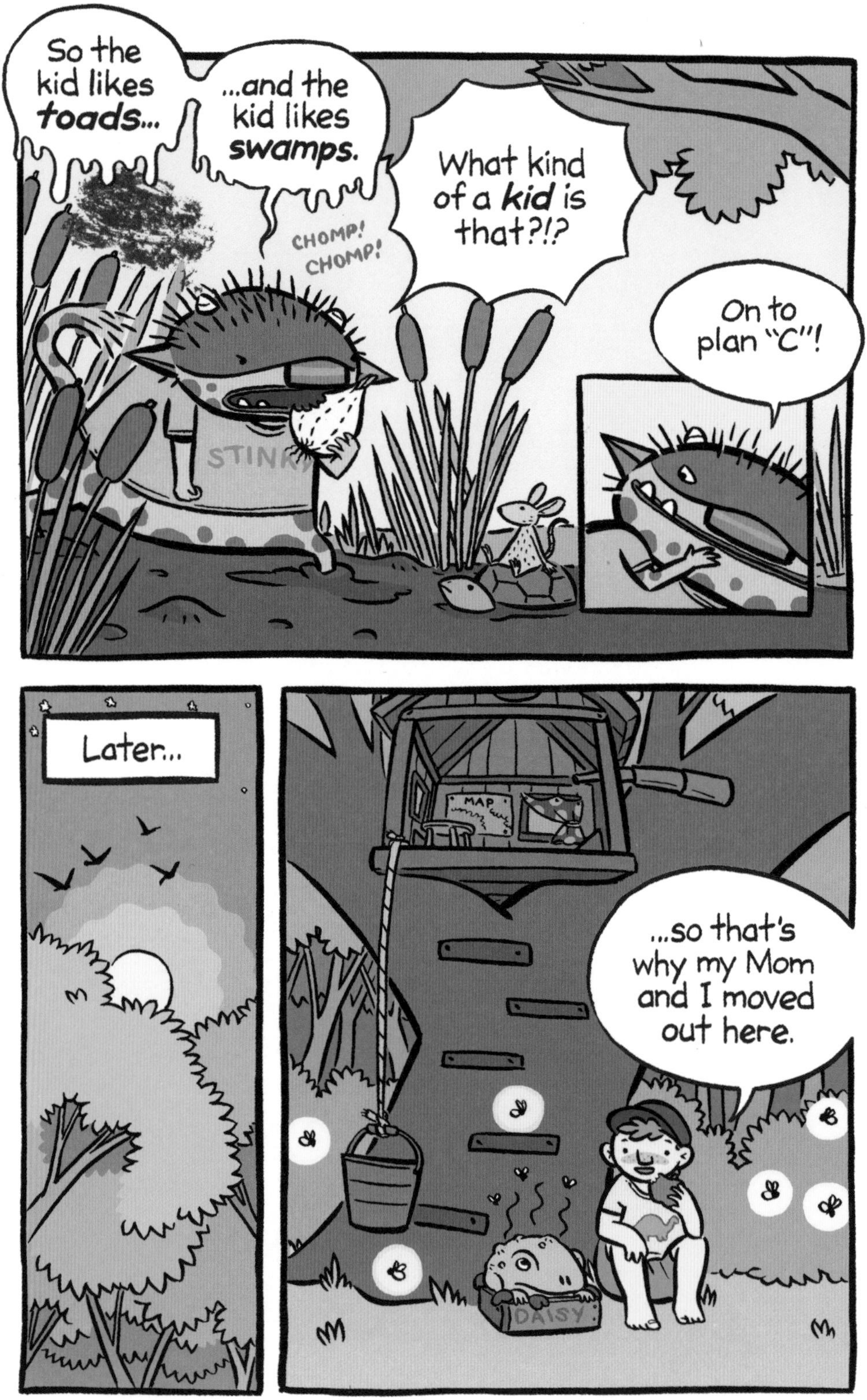

So the kid likes **toads**...
...and the kid likes **swamps**.
CHOMP! CHOMP!
What kind of a **kid** is that?!?
STINKY
On to plan "C"!
Later...
MAP
...so that's why my Mom and I moved out here.
DAISY

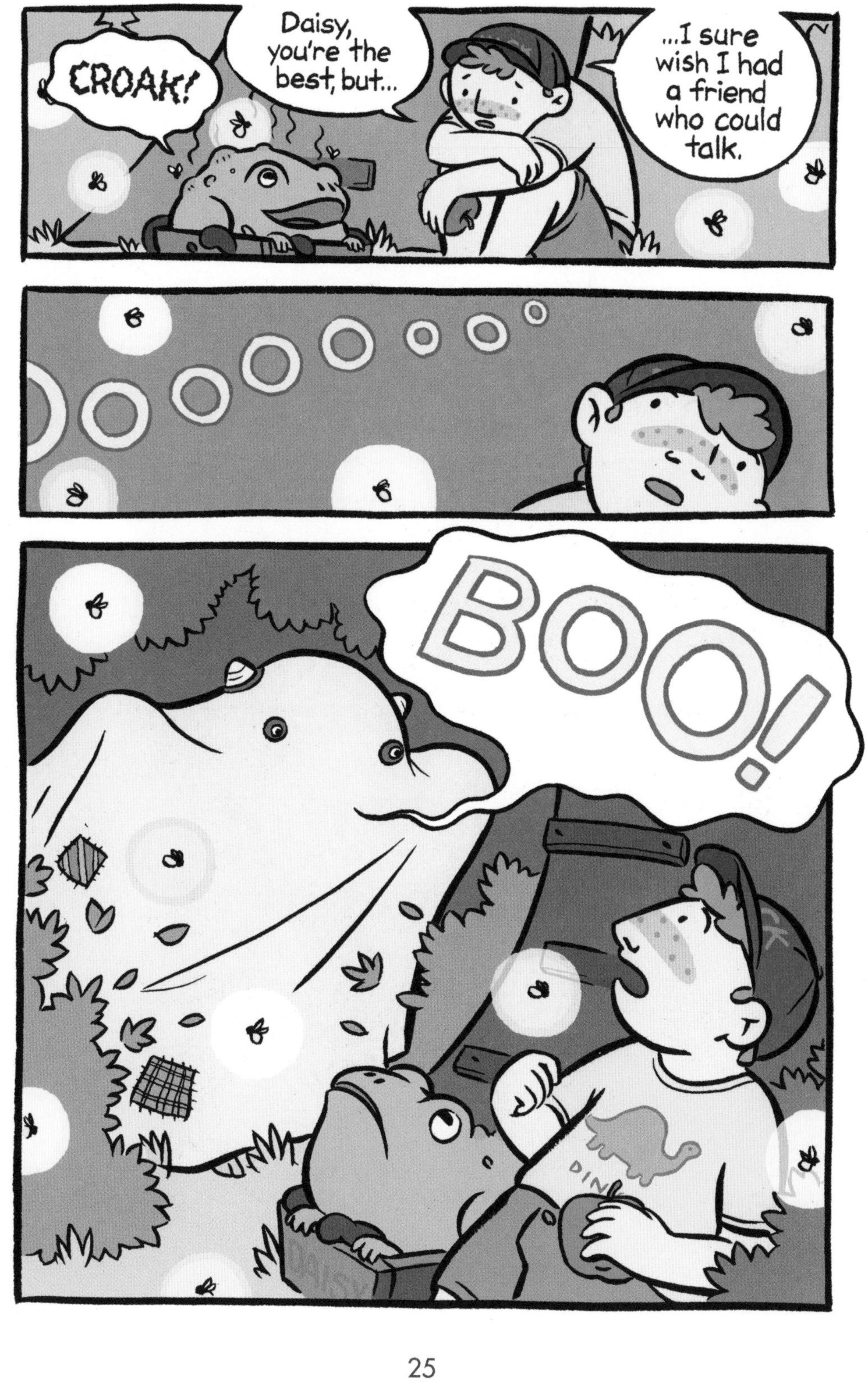
CROAK!
Daisy, you're the best, but...
...I sure wish I had a friend who could talk.
BOO!

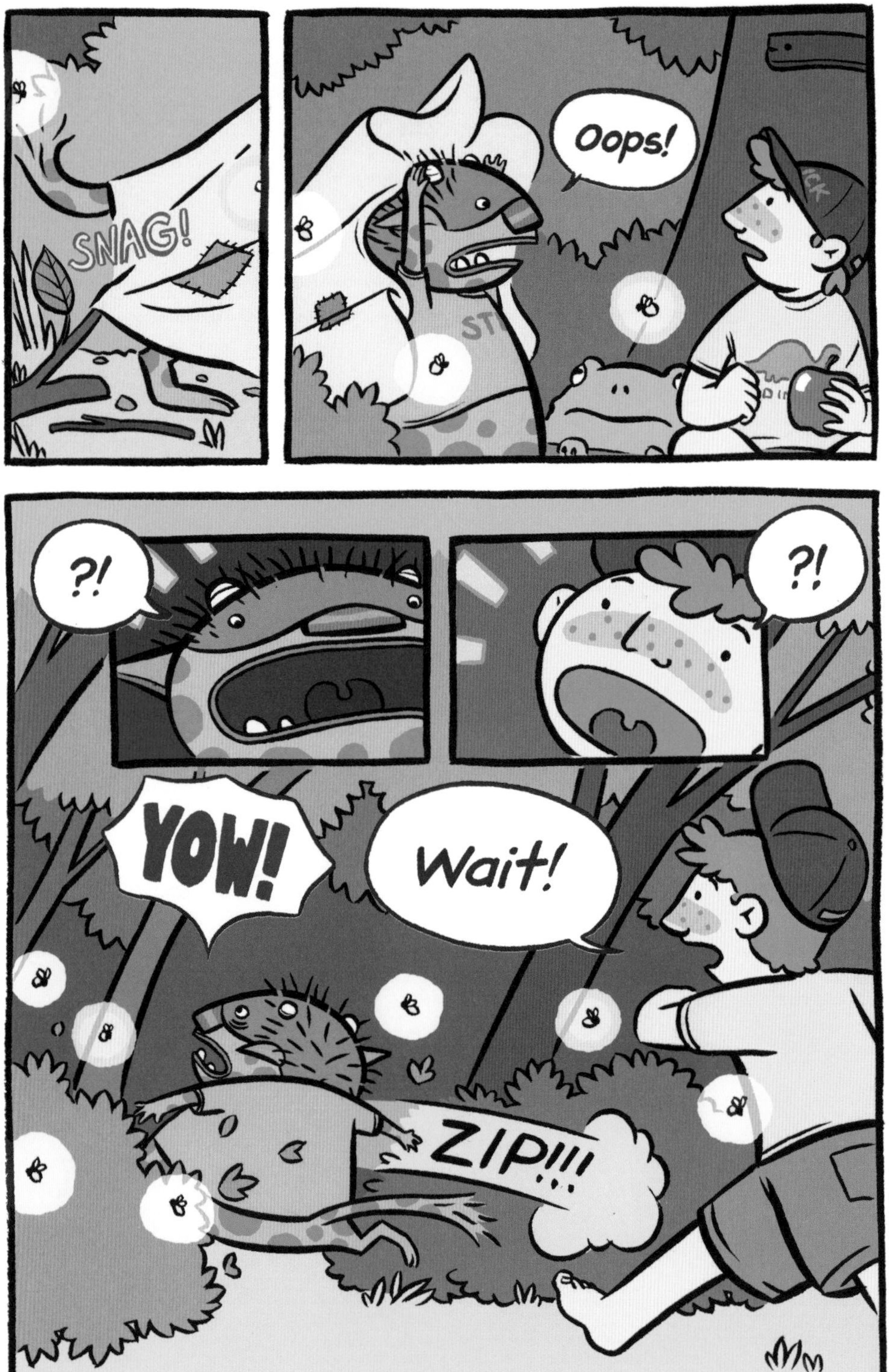
SNAG!
Oops!
?!
?!
YOW!
Wait!
ZIP!!!

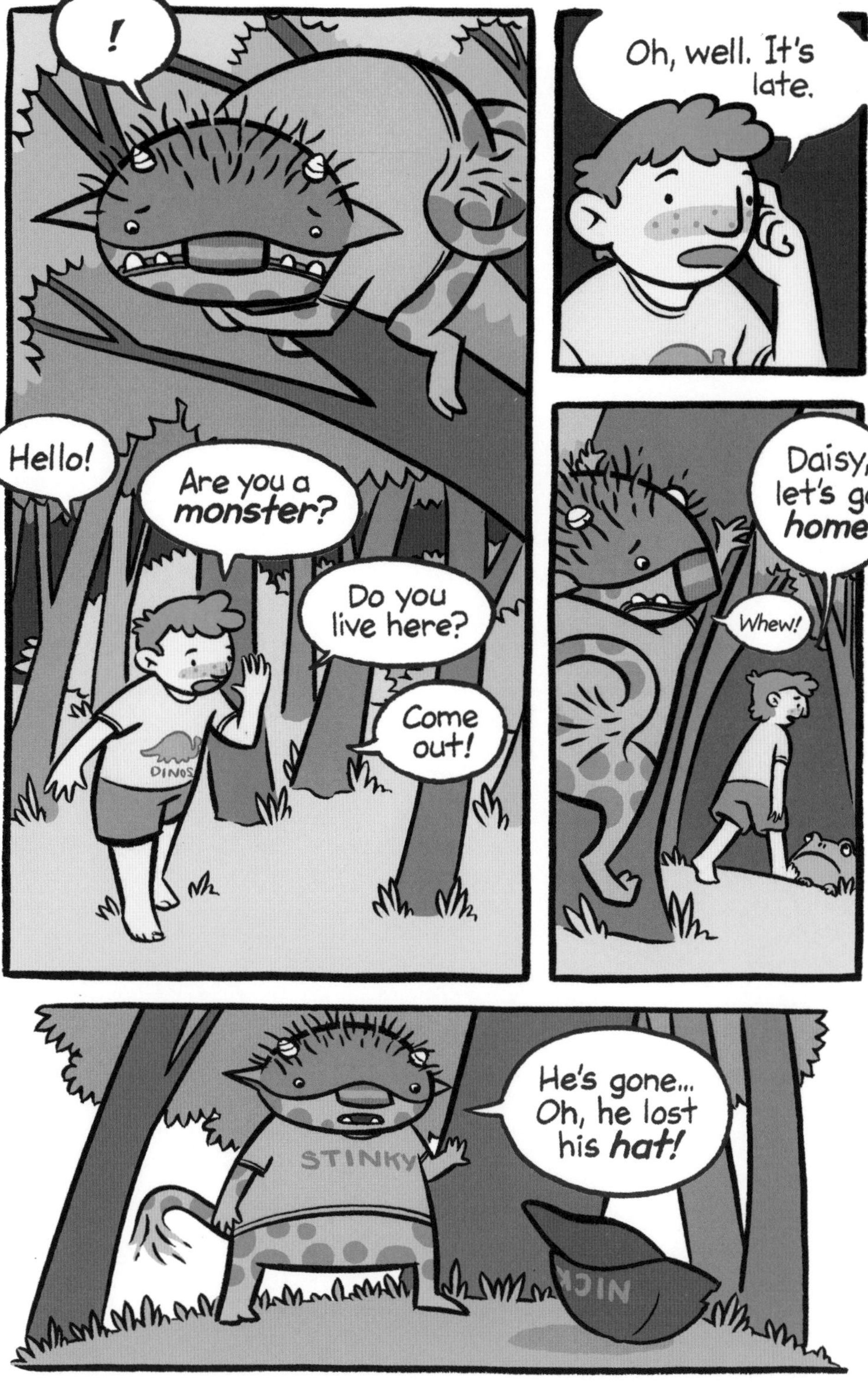
!
Oh, well. It's late.
Hello!
Are you a **monster?**
Do you live here?
Come out!
DINOS
Daisy, let's go **home.**
Whew!
He's gone... Oh, he lost his ***hat!***
STINKY
NICK

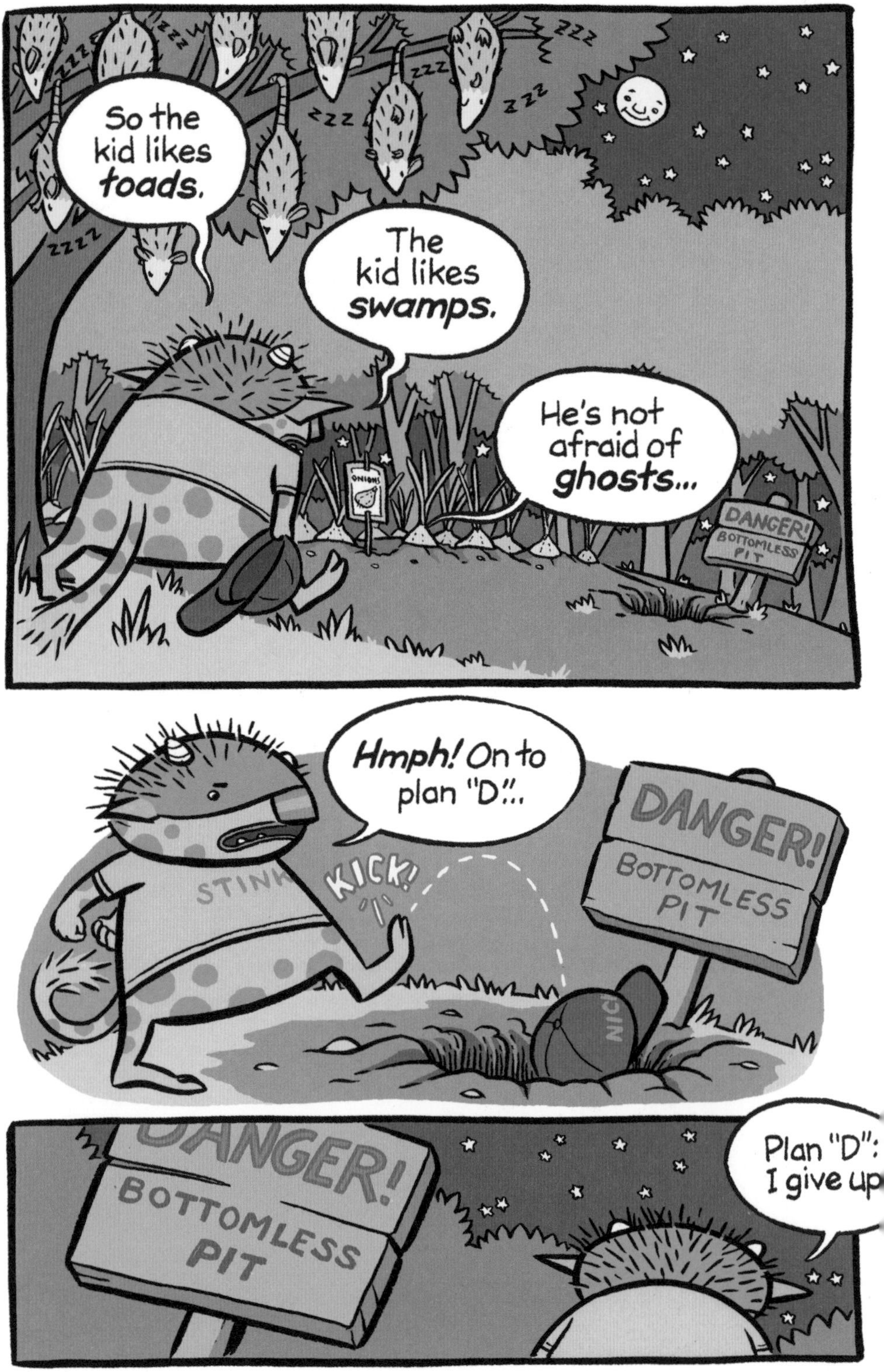
So the kid likes *toads.*
The kid likes *swamps.*
ONIONS
He's not afraid of *ghosts...*
DANGER!
BOTTOMLESS PIT
Hmph! On to plan "D"...
STINK
KICK!
DANGER!
BOTTOMLESS PIT
NIC
DANGER!
BOTTOMLESS PIT
Plan "D": I give up

CHAPTER THREE

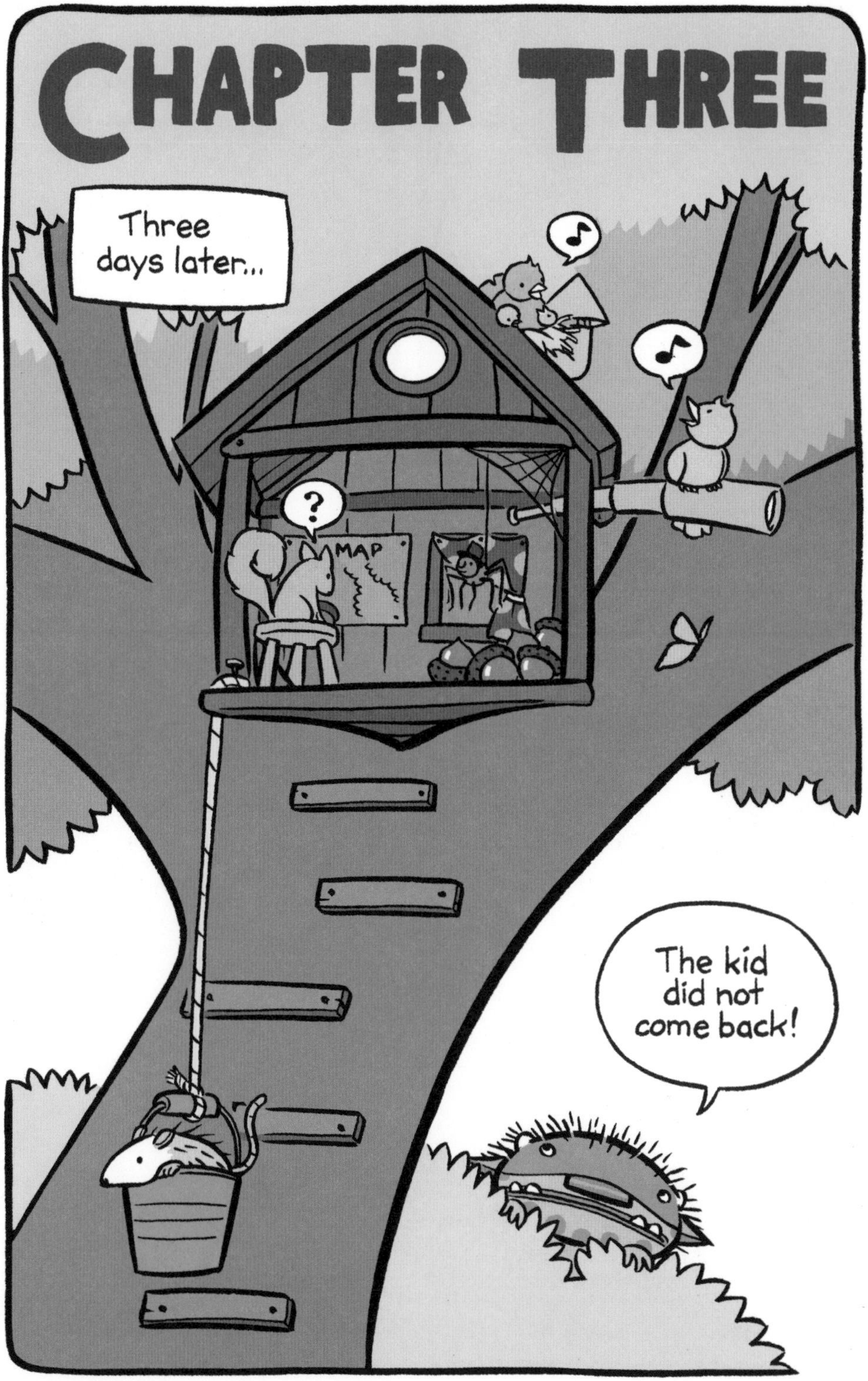
Three days later...
?
MAP
The kid did not come back!

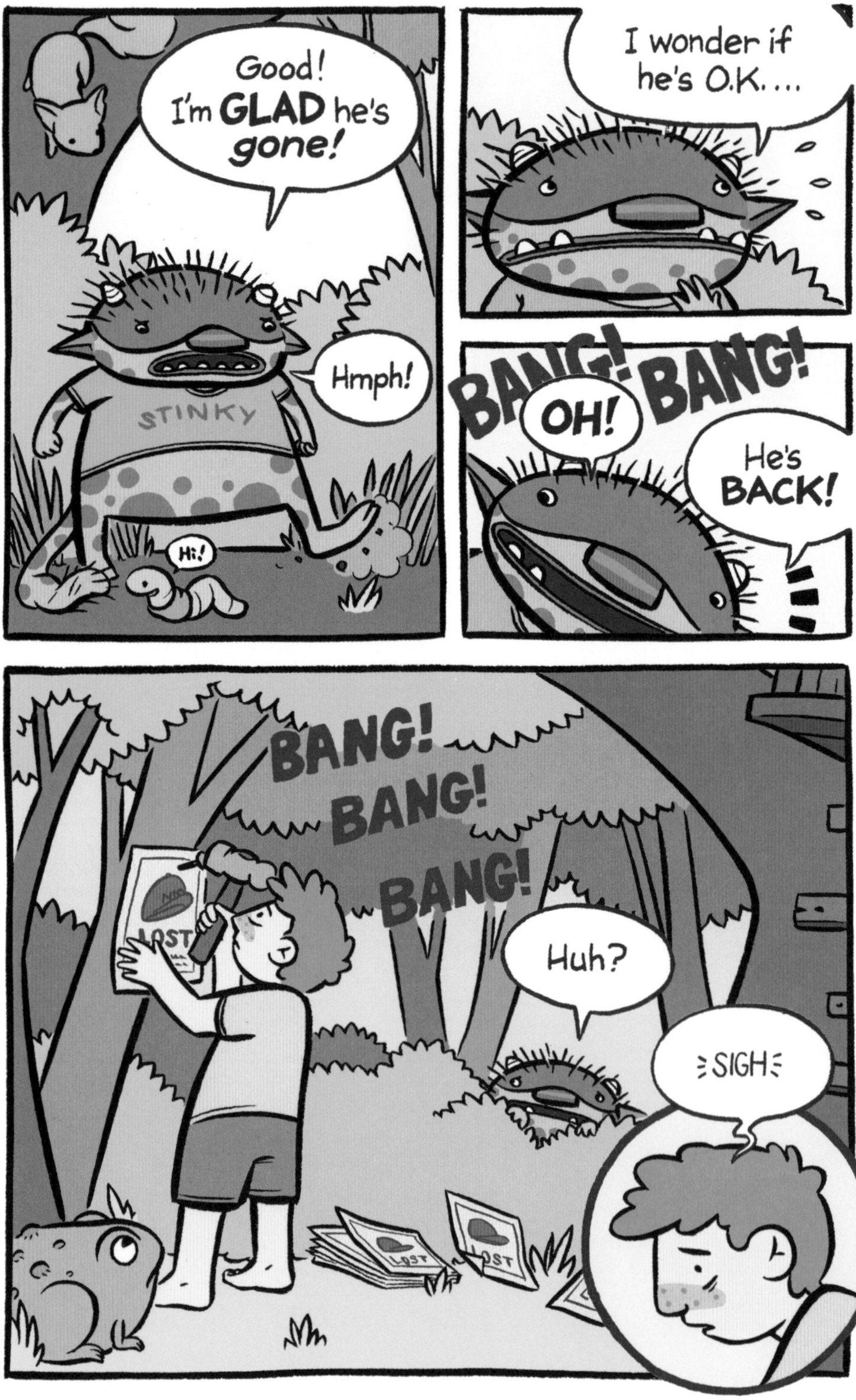
Good! I'm **GLAD** he's *gone!*
Hmph!
STINKY
Hi!
I wonder if he's O.K....
BANG!
OH!
BANG!
He's **BACK!**
BANG!
BANG!
BANG!
LOST
Huh?
SIGH
LOST
LOST

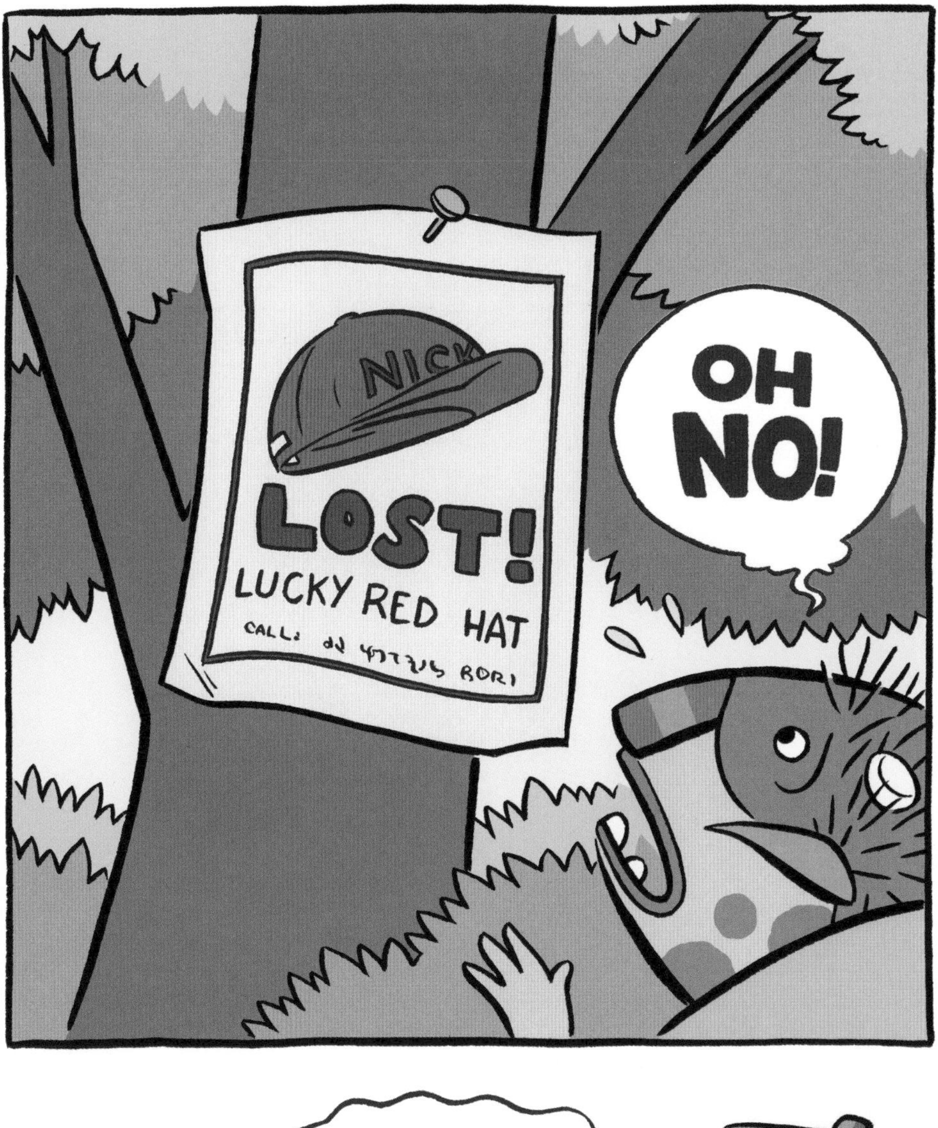
NICK
LOST!
LUCKY RED HAT
OH NO!

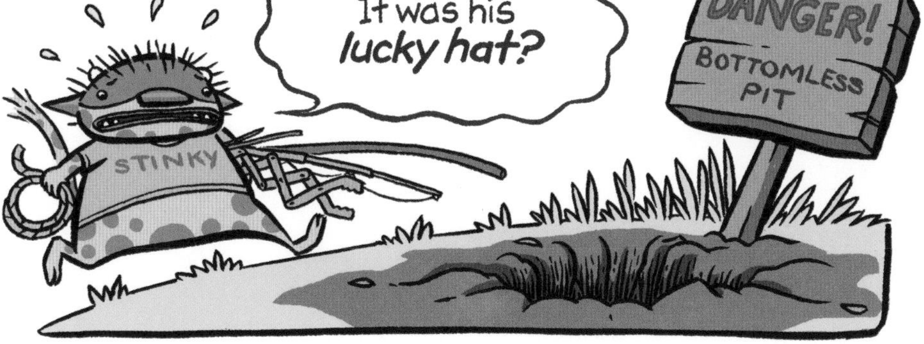
STINKY
It was his *lucky hat?*
DANGER!
BOTTOMLESS PIT

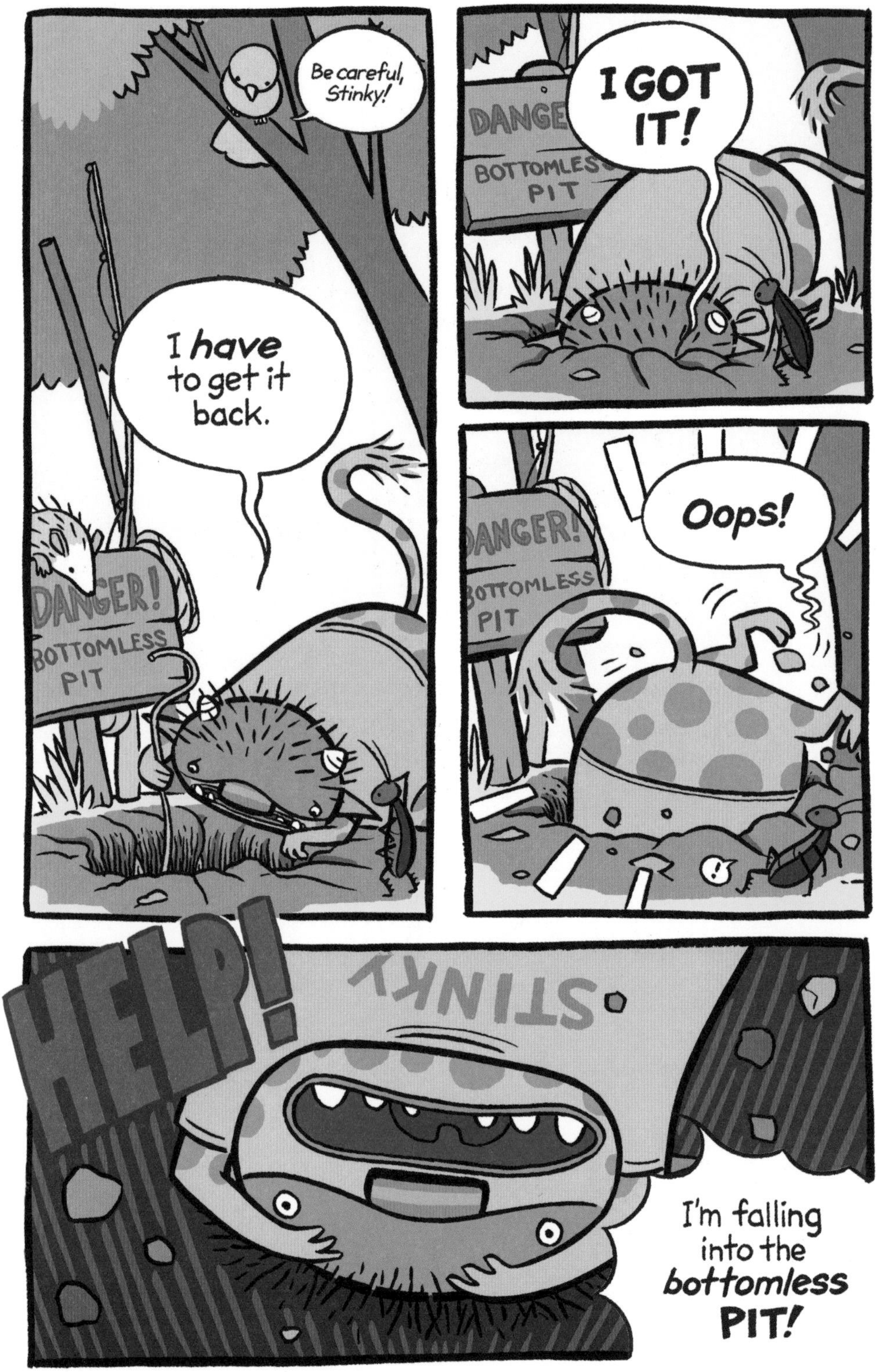
Be careful, Stinky!
I *have* to get it back.
DANGER! BOTTOMLESS PIT
DANGE BOTTOMLESS PIT
I GOT IT!
DANGER! BOTTOMLESS PIT
Oops!
HELP!
STINKY
I'm falling into the *bottomless* **PIT!**

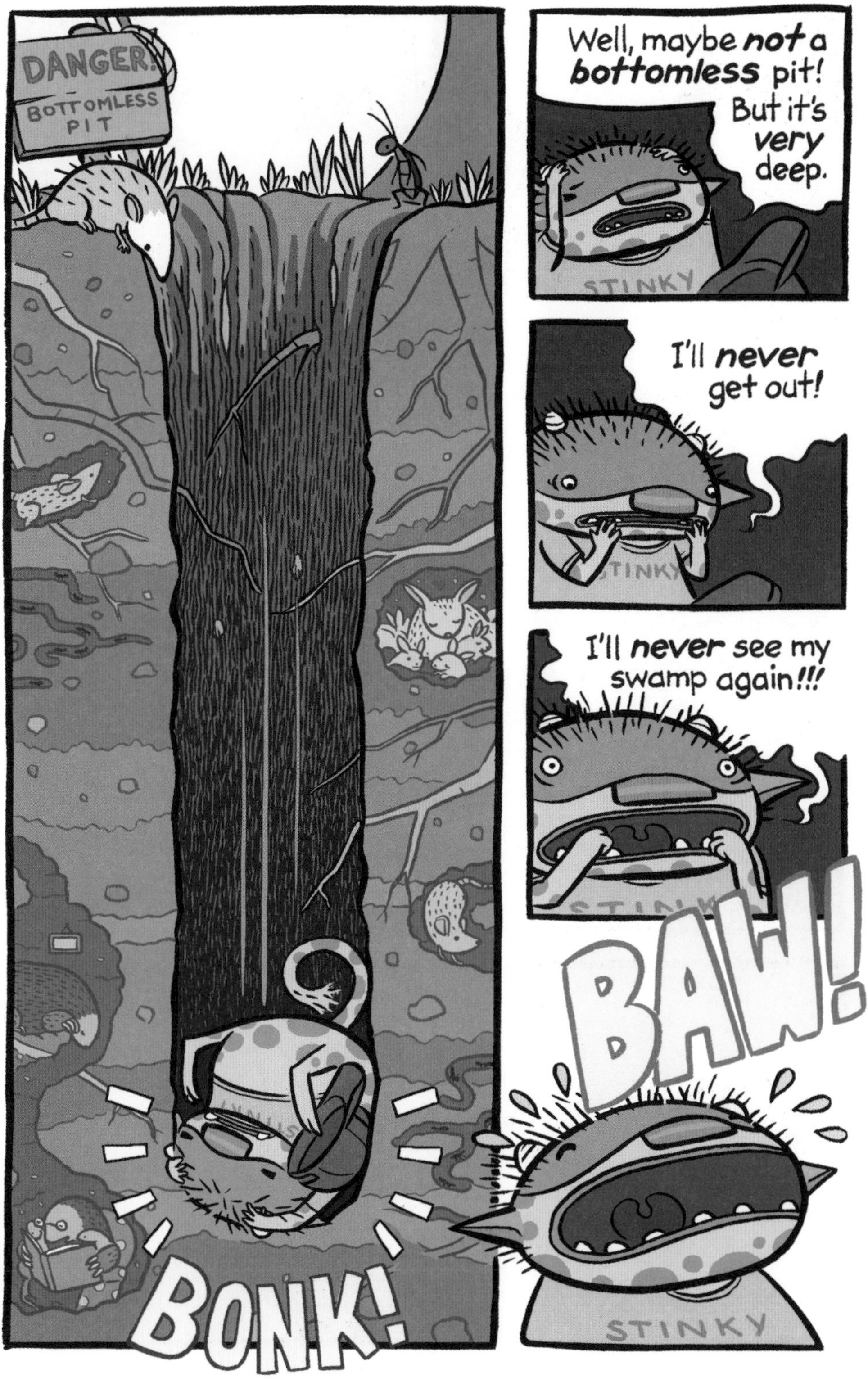
DANGER!
BOTTOMLESS PIT
BONK!
Well, maybe not a bottomless pit!
But it's very deep.
STINKY
I'll never get out!
I'll never see my swamp again!!!
BAW!
STINKY

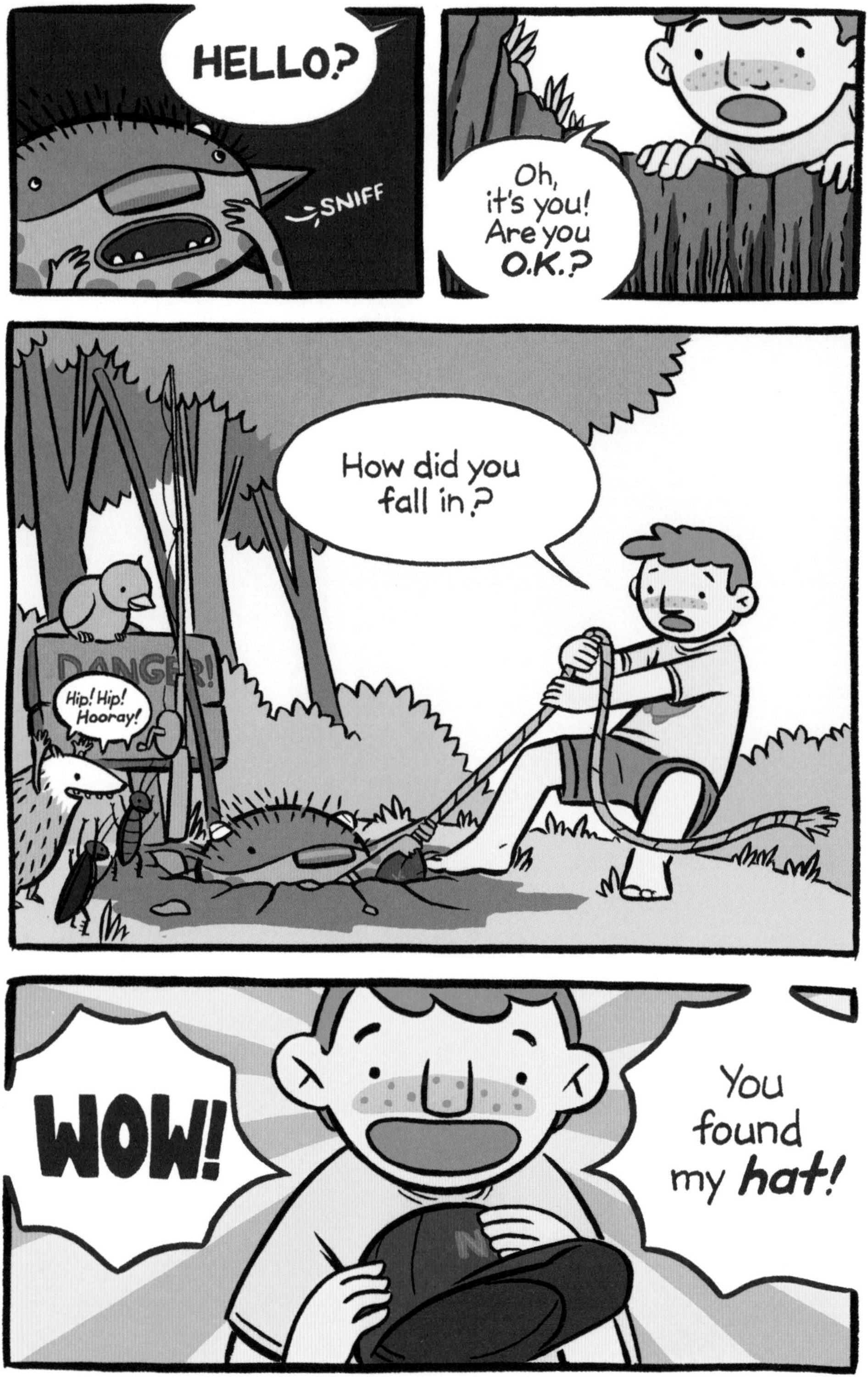
HELLO?
SNIFF
Oh, it's you! Are you O.K.?
How did you fall in?
DANGER!
Hip! Hip! Hooray!
WOW!
You found my hat!

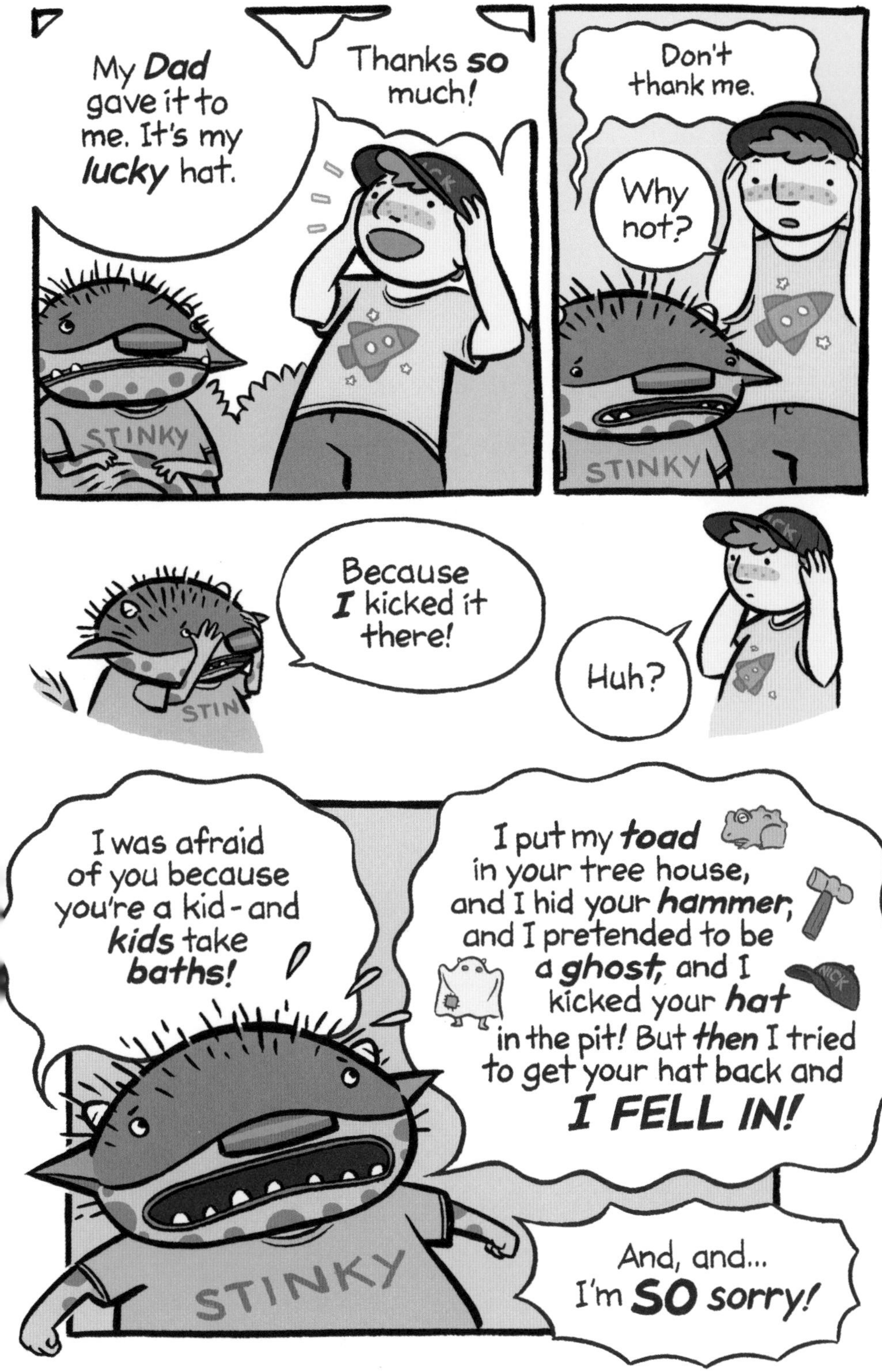
My Dad gave it to me. It's my lucky hat.
Thanks so much!
NICK
STINKY
Don't thank me.
Why not?
STINKY
Because I kicked it there!
STIN
NICK
Huh?
I was afraid of you because you're a kid - and kids take baths!
I put my toad in your tree house, and I hid your hammer, and I pretended to be a ghost, and I kicked your hat in the pit! But then I tried to get your hat back and I FELL IN!
NICK
STINKY
And, and... I'm SO sorry!

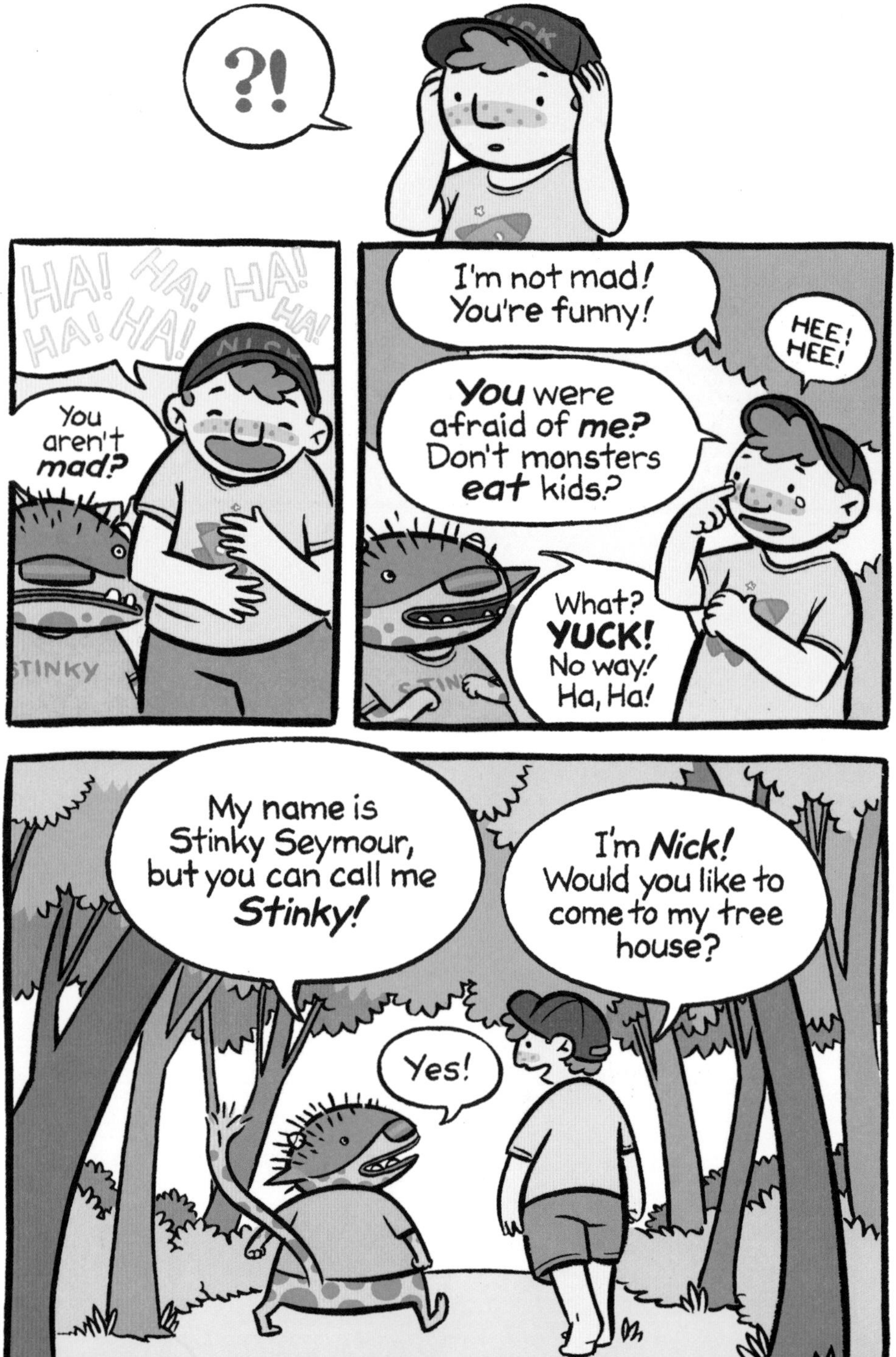
?!
HA! HA! HA! HA! HA! HA!
You aren't *mad?*
NICK
STINKY
I'm not mad! You're funny!
HEE! HEE!
You were afraid of ***me?*** Don't monsters ***eat*** kids?
What? **YUCK!** No way! Ha, Ha!
My name is Stinky Seymour, but you can call me ***Stinky!***
I'm *Nick!* Would you like to come to my tree house?
Yes!

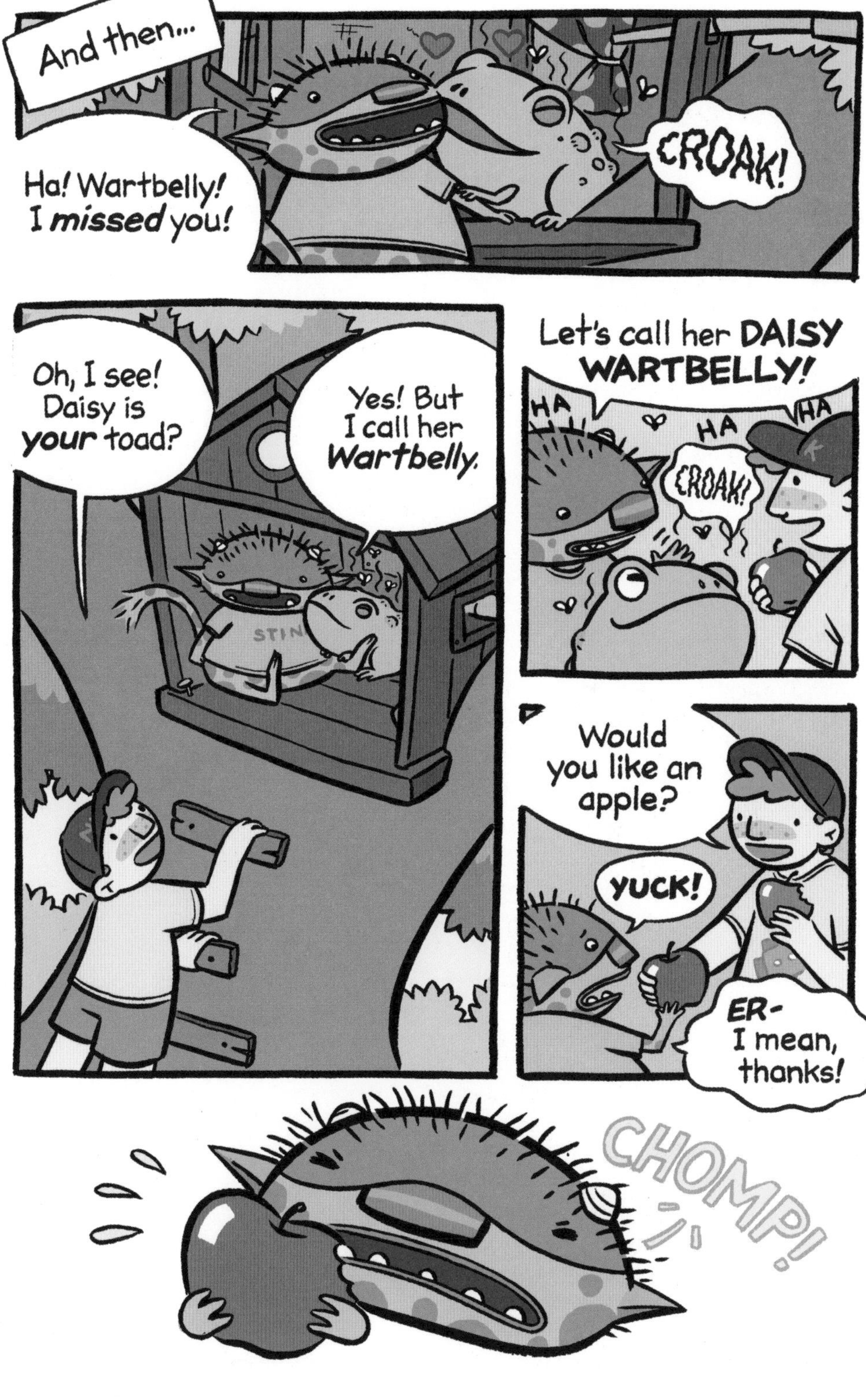
And then...
Ha! Wartbelly! I *missed* you!
CROAK!
Oh, I see! Daisy is **your** toad?
Yes! But I call her ***Wartbelly.***
STIN
Let's call her **DAISY WARTBELLY!**
HA
HA
HA
CROAK!
Would you like an apple?
YUCK!
ER- I mean, thanks!
CHOMP!

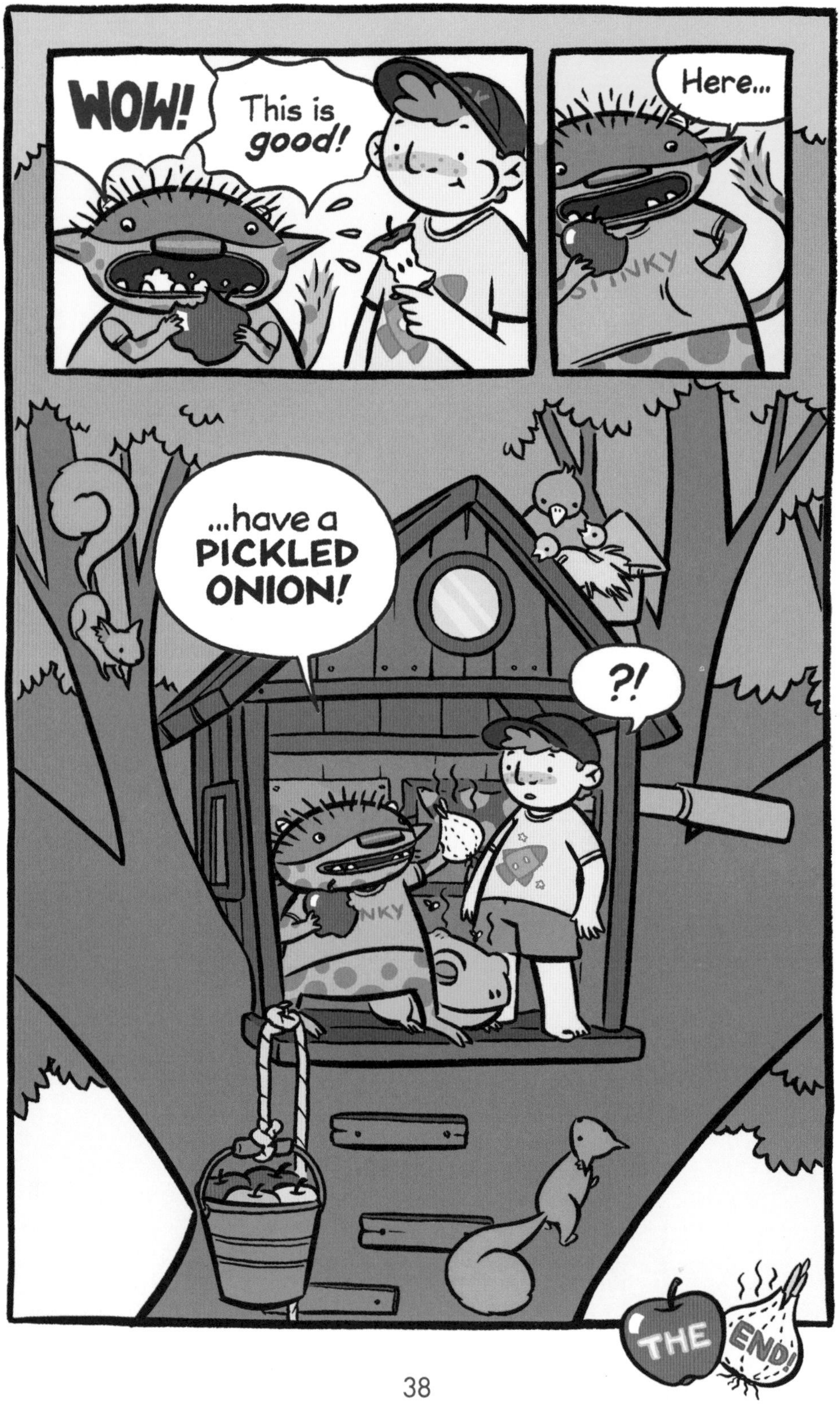
WOW!
This is good!
Here...
...have a PICKLED ONION!
?!
STINKY
THE END!

HOW TO "TOON INTO READING"
in a few simple steps:

Our goal is to get kids reading—and we know kids LOVE comics. We publish award-winning early readers in comics form for elementary and early middle school, and present them in three levels.

1 FIND THE RIGHT BOOK

Veteran teacher Cindy Rosado tells what makes a good book for beginning and struggling readers alike: "A vetted vocabulary, plenty of picture clues, repetition, and a clear and compelling story. Also, the book shouldn't be too easy—or the reader won't learn, but neither should it be too hard—or he or she may get discouraged."

The TOON INTO READING!™ program is designed for beginning readers and works wonders with reluctant readers.

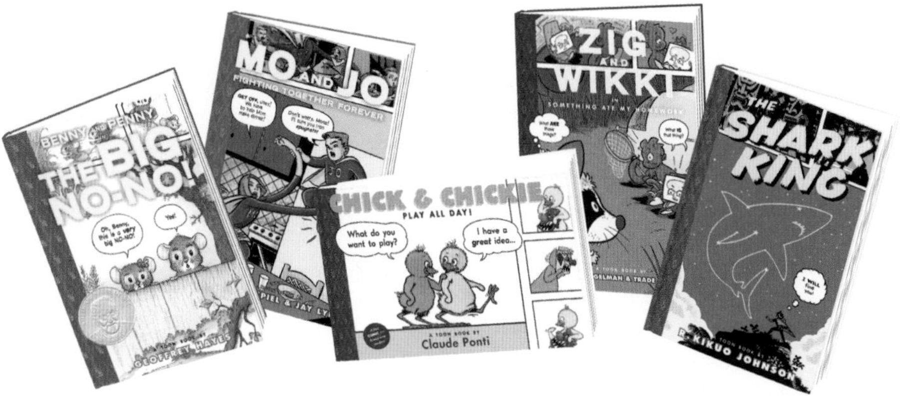

BENNY AND PENNY
THE BIG NO-NO!
MO AND JO
FIGHTING TOGETHER FOREVER
ZIG AND WIKKI
SOMETHING ATE MY HOMEWORK
CHICK & CHICKIE
PLAY ALL DAY!
What do you want to play?
I have a great idea...
A TOON BOOK BY
Claude Ponti
THE SHARK KING
KIKUO JOHNSON

2 TAKE TIME WITH SILENT PANELS

Comics use panels to mark time, and silent panels count. Look and "read" even when there are no words. Often, humor is all in the timing!

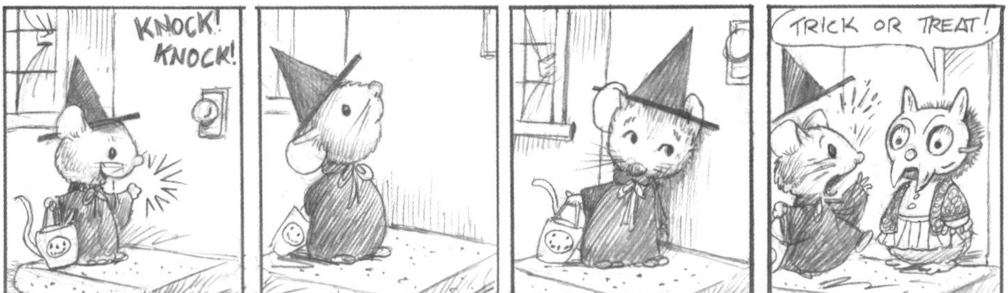

KNOCK! KNOCK!
TRICK OR TREAT!

What works?

Keep your fingertip below the character that is speaking.

3 GUIDE YOUNG READERS

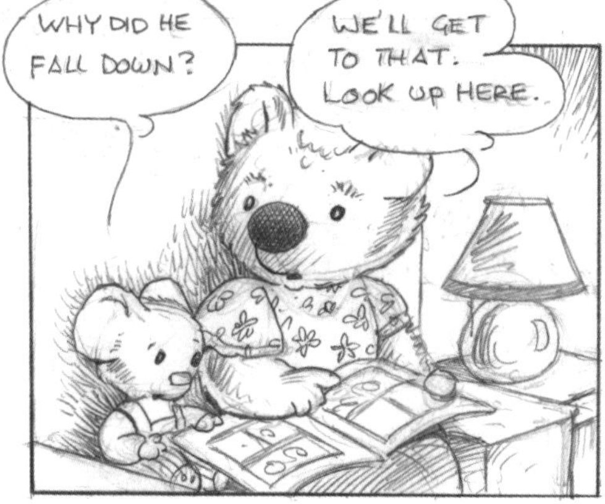
WHY DID HE FALL DOWN?
WE'LL GET TO THAT. LOOK UP HERE.

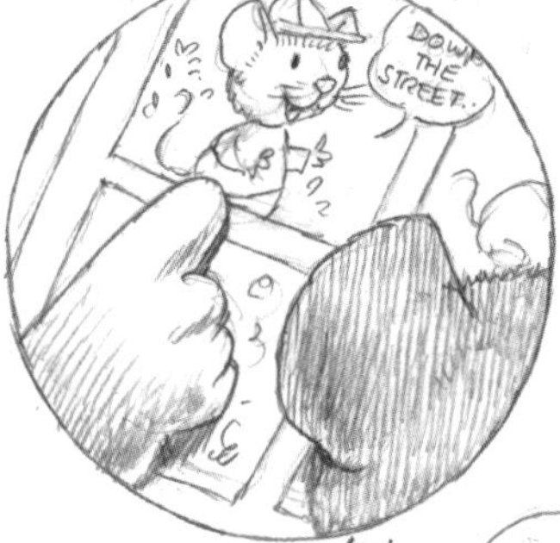
DOWN THE STREET.

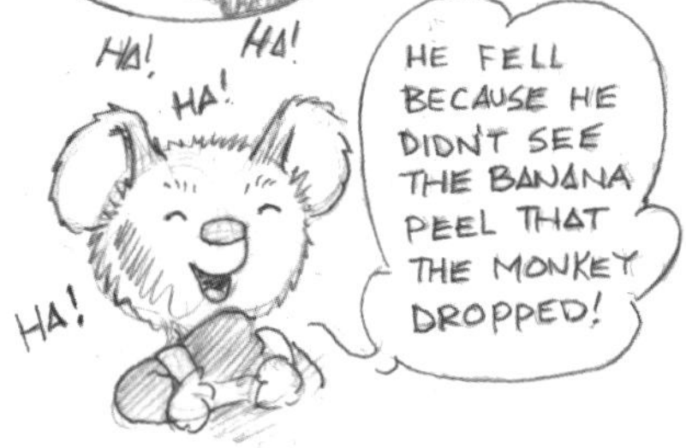
HA! HA! HA! HA!
HE FELL BECAUSE HE DIDN'T SEE THE BANANA PEEL THAT THE MONKEY DROPPED!

4 LET THE PICTURES TELL THE STORY

In a comic, you can often read the story even if you don't know all the words. Encourage young readers to tell you what's happening based on the facial expressions and body language.

5 GET OUT THE CRAYONS

Kids see the hand of the author in a comic and it makes them want to tell their own stories. Encourage them to talk, write and draw!

Get kids talking, and you'll be surprised at how perceptive they are about pictures.

6 LET THEM GUESS

Comics provide a large amount of context for the words, so let young readers make informed guesses, and don't over-correct. In this panel, the artist shows a pirate ship, two pirate hats, and two pirate flags the first time the word "PIRATE" is introduced.

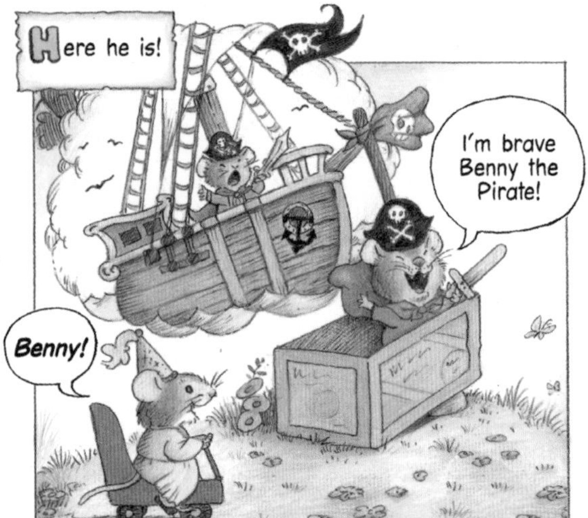
Here he is!
I'm brave Benny the Pirate!
Benny!